D1472293

DATE DUE			
JUL 8 '92			
SEP 24 '92	# 601		
NOV 21 '92			
AUG 10 '94			

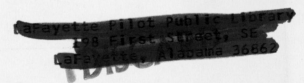

Dolby AND THE
Woof-Off

Dolby AND THE
Woof-Off

BARBARA STEINER

ILLUSTRATED BY
EILEEN CHRISTELOW

Morrow Junior Books
New York

Book design by Karen Palinko

Text copyright © 1991 by Barbara Steiner
Illustrations copyright © 1991 by Eileen Christelow
Inquiries should be addressed to
William Morrow and Company, Inc.,
105 Madison Avenue, New York, N.Y. 10016.

Printed in the United States of America.

1 2 3 4 5 6 7 8 9 10

Library of Congress Cataloging-in-Publication Data
Steiner, Barbara A.
Dolby and the woof-off / Barbara Steiner ; illustrated by Eileen Christelow.
p.   cm.
Summary: Bo teaches his dog Dolby some unusual tricks in an
attempt to win the Woof-Off contest.
ISBN 0-688-08435-4
[1. Dogs—Fiction.   2. Dogs—Training—Fiction.   3. Contests—
Fiction.]   I. Christelow, Eileen, ill.   II. Title.
PZ7.S825Do   1991
[E]—dc20   90-21464 CIP AC

For my super agent
and good friend,
Susan Cohen,
with love

—B.S.

Contents

Dolby AND THE Woof-Off

1

The Woof-Off

"If my eye really is lazy," asked Bo, "what will the doctor do about it?"

Bo Dibbs skipped to keep up with his older brother, Oliver, and their mother, who walked briskly toward the eye clinic. Mrs. Dibbs had left work early so she could take the boys to see Dr. Norbert. Oliver, who wore glasses, needed a regular checkup. One of Bo's eyes was acting funny, so Mrs. Dibbs got him an appointment at the same time.

"Keep it after school?" suggested Ollie. "Take away TV privileges?"

"Make it do push-ups?" Bo tried to joke, as if seeing Dr. Norbert was nothing, but to tell the truth, he was feeling scared.

Ollie had his checkup first. While he waited for his turn—alone, since his mother had gone in with Ollie—

Bo tried not to worry. He hoped Dr. Norbert would say just that he had to have glasses. He wouldn't mind getting glasses. Glasses hadn't stopped Ollie from being the smartest, most fun brother anyone could have. They hadn't stopped Ollie from being famous. Ollie had talked to the governor on the phone twice this past winter. He'd been on a school program with the governor after he'd gotten stegosaurus elected Colorado state fossil.

Bo certainly wasn't afraid of Dr. Norbert. He was a neighbor, living right next door to one of Bo's best friends, Alvin Stenboom. Bo often saw the Norberts with their baby daughter, or walking their miniature schnauzer, Truffles. Dolby, the Dibbses' Great Dane and Labrador mix, hated little dogs, so Bo had to watch him carefully when Truffles walked by. One time, Dr. Norbert even had complimented Bo on having such a well-mannered dog. He didn't know that Bo was hanging on to Dolby, threatening to ground him if he chased Truffles one more time.

"Hi, Bo." Sheri Longholtz skipped into the waiting room with her mother, interrupting Bo's thinking. "What are you doing here all alone?"

"Oh, I'm not alone. My brother is having his checkup. I have an appointment, too, though. My mom thinks my eye is getting lazy."

Sheri laughed and peered at Bo's eyes. "Which one? What will you do about it? Send it to aerobics class?"

Bo raised his eyebrows up and down and moved his

2

eyes from side to side, as if they were exercising. "It's my right eye," he told her.

Mrs. Dibbs came back before Bo and Sheri could visit any more. They were both in Mrs. Henderson's first-grade classroom. Bo liked Sheri. He thought maybe he'd like to play with her some this summer.

It was Ollie's turn to wait while Bo had his checkup. After putting Bo in a big chair, making him read eye charts, and looking into his eyes with all sorts of strange machines, Dr. Norbert made a decision. Bo's joke about push-ups was close to the truth.

"You do indeed have strabismus, sometimes called lazy eye, Bo," said Dr. Norbert. "That means that one of the muscles in your eye is weak. We have to strengthen the muscle, make it work harder so your eye will stop turning in."

Now Bo imagined dressing his eye in track shoes and running shorts or, funnier yet, walking it on a leash as he did with Dolby. He smiled and tried to relax. "How can you do that, Dr. Norbert?"

"You'll do it, Bo." Dr. Norbert opened a drawer. "I'm going to put a patch over the good eye. Then the lazy eye will have to do all the work and get stronger." While he talked, Dr. Norbert fitted a black patch over Bo's left eye. It was held in place by a strap of elastic around Bo's head.

"How long do I have to wear this thing?" Bo asked, touching the patch. He could already hear everyone at school laughing at him.

"Probably only a few weeks," Dr. Norbert assured Bo. "We'll keep a check on it. When your eyes are working together well, we can take it off. Don't be surprised if you have to have glasses after the patch comes off, though."

Bo wanted glasses now. He didn't want a black eye patch. He wished he could go out the back door. Slowly, he walked into the waiting room while Mrs. Dibbs paid their bill. Glancing around, he was relieved to see that Sheri and her mom were gone.

"Hey, that's neat, Bo," Ollie said. "You look like a pirate."

Bo figured Ollie was trying to make him feel better about looking funny. In the car, Bo explained about having a lazy eye, until they came to a stop.

"Do we have to go in the store?" Bo didn't want everyone in the whole world to see him until he got used to the patch.

"Your father will be late tonight." Mrs. Dibbs held the car door open, insisting that Bo get out. "I'll have time to fix a good dinner for a change. I'm hungry for something with a barbecue sauce."

Everyone in the grocery store stared at him. Bo couldn't wait to get home. The minute he got out of the car, Dolby barked and barked.

"See, even Dolby thinks I look funny," Bo complained. "It's me, Dolby. See." Bo lifted the eye patch to show Dolby both eyes. Then he popped it back in place.

Dolby crouched down, peered at Bo, and barked

again. Finally, he jumped up, rested his front paws on Bo's shoulders, and licked his face.

"He knows you, silly," Ollie said, and disappeared into the house with a load of groceries.

Bo untied Dolby and sat beside him on the back doorstep, his arm around the big dog. "I feel really stupid, Dolby. I know everyone will laugh at me."

Before Bo could decide whether it would be better to run away with Dolby and live at Sawhill Ponds east of Boulder or hide in his room until his eye was retrained, the screen door slammed. It was Ollie.

"Here, Bo. Captain Blood sails the mighty seas, looking for ships to vanquish." Ollie was always using big words. Bo was more interested in the black construction-paper hat Ollie was holding. There was even a skull and crossbones painted on it.

Ollie set the hat on Bo's curly blond hair. Then he waved a cardboard sword, swishing the air. "On guard. Avast, you landlubbers!"

"Hey, neat." Bo took the sword and waved it at Dolby. He struck a fighting pose. "Avast, Dolby."

Dolby jumped up and barked. He was ready for any game. Bo pushed open the screen door and leaped into the kitchen, Dolby at his heels.

"Avast, Mom. What's to eat?" Bo laughed when Dolby barked. He was saying *Me, too.* Bo thought Dolby was probably the smartest dog in the whole world.

Mrs. Dibbs threw her hands in the air and pretended to scream. "If you won't make me walk the plank, you can have an apple."

"And my trusty dog?" Bo frowned and snarled, waving the sword.

"A Woofies. Please, please, give him a Woofies." Mrs. Dibbs smiled and turned to stir the carrot cake she'd started for dinner.

Grabbing an apple, Bo opened a low corner-cabinet door. He reached for a Woofies Doggie Snack. "Speak, Dolby, speak."

"*Woof-woof. Woof-woof.*" Dolby knew this trick perfectly. He sat on his haunches and responded with his low bark.

"Good dog." Bo patted Dolby and tossed the snack into the air for Dolby to catch. He never missed. *Slurp. Crunch.* The Woofies was gone.

"Can Alvin and Gary come over until dinner is ready?" Bo asked, biting into the crisp apple.

He could see his reflection in the glass door of the oven. He trusted his best friends not to laugh now that he had the pirate hat. He looked pretty neat. When Mom nodded yes, Bo called them from the kitchen phone. He was sitting on the back steps and had just finished his apple when they rounded the big tree in the backyard.

"Captain Blood is looking for ships to vanish," shouted Bo, jumping up and brandishing his sword.

"Hey, great." Alvin stopped and stared at Bo. "Who made the hat? I want one, too."

"Neat eye patch," said Gary. "You really look like a pirate. I want one."

Bo didn't tell his friends that his eye patch was real

until Ollie had made both Alvin and Gary a hat and patch and a cardboard sword.

"I didn't know I was getting into all this work," Ollie complained. He smiled a little when he said it, so Bo knew he wasn't really mad.

Bo cut out a black paper patch for Dolby and taped it over one of his eyes. Dolby tolerated the patch for about ten seconds, then ducked his head and pawed it off.

"Oh, well, I guess pirate dogs need to see well to help us find our enemies," Bo declared. Now fully equipped, he and his friends took off to terrorize the neighborhood until dinnertime.

"How long do we get to eat with a pirate?" Mr. Dibbs asked that night at the dinner table.

Bo already had explained to Alice, his big sister, about the patch. "Dr. Norbert didn't know," Bo answered his father. "He'll check my eye every two weeks."

"I think it's kind of romantic." Alice was almost finished with ninth grade. Ollie said she had two categories for life—romantic or grossed-out. Bo was glad she didn't say he looked grossed-out, but he didn't want to look romantic, either. Alice giggled, and Bo stuck out his tongue as she went to cut the cake.

"Listen to this, Bo." Ollie held up an article he'd clipped from that day's newspaper. He and his father had finished clearing the table and everyone was having dessert.

"Woofies Dog Food is sponsoring a national competition that's open to all dogs. They're looking for a dog to star in their commercials. More important than looks," he read, "the dog must display a great *woof*. The contest will be narrowed to a small number of competitors through regional events. The Rocky Mountain competition will be held on May twenty-fifth in Boulder. Regional winners will attend the finals in Cincinnati, Ohio, all expenses paid by Woofies Dog Food Company. It gives the rules right here, but it says there's an entry blank on the Woofies bag. They're calling it a Woof-Off."

"Wow! The contest is right here in Boulder?" Bo jumped straight up off his chair and ran to get the dog food. Dolby, who sat underneath Bo because he was the messiest, came to life.

"Woof-woof," Dolby barked.

"See? Dolby loves the idea," Bo said. "Can we enter Dolby, Dad, can we?" Bo looked at the entry blank and rules.

"It would take a long time to train Dolby, more than the five weeks you have. Dogs in television commercials have to do more than roll over and speak."

"Woof-woof." Dolby knew the word *speak*.

Bo hugged the big dog. "Sit, Dolby, sit. See, he knows *sit*." Bo had to push Dolby's haunches down twice. He knew the attention was on him, and he was too excited to sit. "Ollie and I can train him in five weeks. I know we can. Ollie can do anything."

"I'm sorry, Bo. I don't have time to train Dolby."

Ollie folded the newspaper clipping. "I'm using all my spare time to raise money for the Reptile House at the Denver Zoo. I just showed you the clipping because I thought it was a neat idea."

"Then I'll do it by myself. Can I, Dad? Can I, Mom?" Bo begged. "Give me a chance. You have to."

Mr. and Mrs. Dibbs looked at each other. Mrs. Dibbs shrugged. Mr. Dibbs smiled. "I guess it won't hurt to try. May twenty-fifth is the day of the solar eclipse, though. I won't be able to help you. I'll be in Mexico."

"I might be able to help . . . a little," Ollie added, smiling at Bo.

"Why do you have to go to Mexico for the eclipse?" asked Bo. "Why can't you see it right here?"

"Each solar eclipse has a path, Bo, and we have to be in that path to see the total eclipse. There'll be a partial eclipse this far north, but the direct path is across Hawaii and Mexico. It'll last six minutes this time."

"You're going to Mexico for something that'll last six minutes?" said Alice.

"Sometimes the duration is only two minutes." Mr. Dibbs was a solar physicist. He studied the activity of the sun—its flares and eclipses—and the effects of radiation. "The sun is very active just now. Some scientists are trying to find out whether this extra activity is affecting our weather."

"Something is. It seems really hot for April." Mrs. Dibbs started clearing the dishes. "Bo, I think I have new computers coming in for testing the week of May twenty-fifth. I don't know whether I can get that changed. If they're here, I'll have to work with them all weekend."

Mrs. Dibbs worked for a computer manufacturer. She programmed and tested new computers and often wrote software for them. She also supervised several people who tested the programs.

Bo hardly heard what his mother said. He didn't care about the weather. He raised his eyebrows up and down, reminding himself of the patch. Wearing it no longer seemed to matter, either. All that mattered was entering Dolby in the Woof-Off.

2

A Message from Dolby

After dinner, Bo sat on the back step again with Dolby. He read the article about the Woof-Off over and over. He studied the rules on the entry blank. Funny he hadn't seen it before, but he didn't pay much attention to bags of dog food. Ollie had read the rules at dinner, and Bo had listened, but now he needed to think about each of them.

First, he needed a photo of Dolby. That was easy. He'd ask his dad if he could use his new Polaroid camera.

Second, he had to get a tape recording of Dolby's voice. Maybe, just maybe, if she was in a good mood, Alice would let Bo borrow her boom box. With her baby-sitting money, she'd bought the best one she could find. Not only did it have an AM/FM radio but two tape players. You could copy one tape onto a blank, or you could plug in the tiny microphone and record.

The third part of the contest seemed the hardest. Dolby had to perform for the judges, obey simple commands like *sit* and *stay*. That was no problem. Dolby had been to obedience school. Mrs. Dibbs had insisted on that when they decided to get a dog. But he had to do some special tricks in addition to the usual things dogs know. He had to give a five- to ten-minute program. *Speak* and *roll over* wouldn't even fill five minutes. Bo had to think of some really neat things for Dolby to do.

Ollie had showed Bo how to brainstorm, which meant letting a lot of ideas—even silly or impossible ones—pop out of your head. He was trying to do that when Alice came outside on her way to the movies. She sat on the step beside Bo, holding her hands out so her fingernail polish could finish drying. She had painted each nail a different shade of red. It was kind of pretty, Bo thought—much better than the black-and-pink-striped nails she had worn all last week.

"Bo, millions of dogs will enter the Woof-Off. Have fun entering Dolby, but don't get your hopes up too high." Alice blew on her nails.

"I don't care how many enter." Bo hugged Dolby, who licked his face. "Dolby, the Wonder Dog, will win."

"I hope so, Bo. I'll come and cheer for him if I can." Alice took off as her best friend, Roberta Singer, and her mother pulled into the drive and honked.

Ollie came out just as Alice left. He and his friends Rebecca Sawyer and Frank Ashburn were going to get together. They were working on a play called *Our*

Friend, the Reptile to present in the neighborhood. They planned to charge admission, and the money raised after expenses would go to the Denver Zoo's new Reptile House. Ollie already had told Bo that only fifth graders could take part.

He stopped to offer Bo advice. "Maybe I shouldn't have told you about the contest, Bo. The competition will be really tough. Think how many smart dogs there must be in Boulder, much less the United States."

"I know that, Ollie. I'm not dumb. But Dolby is smart, too. Dolby, the Wonder Dog will win. He'll vanish all the competition."

"Vanquish, Bo, vanquish," Ollie corrected Bo.

"Whatever," Bo said. "Same difference. Dolby will win."

"Hi, Ollie," said Frank, sliding his bike to a stop. "What's up?"

"Oh, nothing. I'll tell you about it later. Come on. Rebecca will wonder where we are." Ollie hopped on his bike and the two boys headed for Rebecca's house.

"It's not nothing," Bo said indignantly. "Is it, Dolby?"

Dolby woofed that he still liked the idea.

Bo was sure he didn't need Ollie's help. Here was something he could do all by himself. He'd show Ollie. He'd become famous just like Ollie; then Ollie would say he was sorry he had thought Dolby couldn't win. His father would realize, too, that Bo could train Dolby to do great tricks.

Taking a deep breath, Bo jumped up. He bowed to

Dolby and, in a loud announcer's voice, said, "Introducing Bo Dibbs, trainer of the Wonder Dog, Dolby, star of stage and screen and television commercials." Hopping two steps to his right to be Bo Dibbs, he bowed while the audience clapped and clapped. They clapped so much, he had to hold up his hand to get them to stop. "Thank you, thank you, ladies and gentlemen. Now let me show you what my dog can do."

Bo would have his eye patch off by then, of course. Dog trainers weren't pirates, or even romantic. They were famous, though. People would beg him to train their dogs. He'd have to check his appointment book to see if he had time. He'd probably make a lot of money, too. Maybe he would even donate a little to some of Ollie's causes.

"What do you think, Dolby?" Bo laughed as Dolby tilted his head sideways and seemed to smile. "I think I'm glad Ollie is too busy to enter the Woof-Off."

On Saturday morning, Mrs. Dibbs asked Alice to wait a couple of hours before leaving the house. Alice grumbled, but she wasn't even dressed. Bo knew it would take her at least two hours to get ready. "I'm going to turn the answering machine on, Alice. Then you and the boys won't have to worry about the phone."

For her birthday, and as an early ninth-grade-graduation gift, Alice had gotten her own telephone. Mom had said it was a present the rest of the family needed, too, since Alice tied up the family telephone too much talking to her friends.

"But what if a call's for me?" complained Ollie. "Someone might call about the play."

"You can listen to the messages. Your father is trying to put together an international team of scientists to view the solar eclipse, so he wants to be certain he gets his calls. If people can't catch him at his office, they might call here."

"I *need* to go to town, Mom. Please promise me you'll be back by ten-thirty or eleven at the latest."

"Yes, I will." Mrs. Dibbs looked over a long list of errands. "I'm trying to arrange all this efficiently."

Alice got paid to baby-sit Ollie and Bo after school every day until Mr. and Mrs. Dibbs got home from work. The only way she could get out of it was if she had a school activity. Then Bo and Ollie had to stop at Mrs. Rumwinkle's house or she would come to their house.

Bo and Ollie loved it when Alice baby-sat. Ollie usually looked after Bo while Alice talked on the phone. Sometimes Alice would bring friends home. They'd lock themselves in Alice's room and laugh and giggle and eat. The boys could do pretty much as they pleased.

Today, Bo had his own list of things to do. His dad had taken a photograph of Dolby the night before. It had turned out pretty neat, Bo thought, looking at it again. Dolby was holding his head sideways, as if to say, "I'm listening. Now what do you want me to say about Woofies?"

Bo needed to make a tape recording of Dolby's bark this morning. The judges would use the photographs and the barks to choose twenty-five finalists for the regional contest. The tape and photo had to be mailed by Monday at the latest. Bo couldn't believe how close he had come to missing out. There must have been an earlier notice of the competition, but even Ollie had overlooked it. Ollie read the newspaper every day, looking for new animal causes and other things that interested him. Bo didn't have that habit, but he planned to start it after this contest was over. There were sure to be movie and TV jobs for a wonder dog and his trainer.

"Can I borrow your tape recorder, Alice?" Bo asked as soon as Mrs. Dibbs left and Ollie had gone to his room. Mr. Dibbs had an appointment at his office to look at some new equipment for measuring solar flares.

"What for?" It was never easy to borrow anything from Alice.

"I have to make a tape of Dolby's woof for the contest."

"I'll help you. This had better not take long, though. I've got better things to do than listen to Dolby barking."

"But think how proud you'll be when Dolby wins," Bo pointed out.

Alice sighed. She went to her room and brought back her boom box and her manicure set. She spread everything out on the kitchen table.

"There's already a blank tape in it, Bo, but you have to pay me for it. Don't forget. All you have to do is turn on the microphone and push the RECORD button."

While Bo and Alice talked, Dolby lay on the floor,

chin on his paws, watching. He glanced up when Bo got out a handful of Woofies Snacks, but he had just eaten a big breakfast of Woofies regular food, and he wasn't hungry. In fact, he usually took a long nap before the day's activities got under way.

Bo wondered how to record Dolby's voice and not his own. Maybe it wouldn't matter. He turned on the mike, put one finger on the RECORD button, and, with the other hand, picked up a Woofies Snack. He showed it to Dolby.

"Speak, Dolby. Speak." Quickly Bo pressed RECORD.

Dolby said nothing.

Bo pressed STOP.

"Speak, Dolby. Speak!" Bo tried again.

"Wuf." Dolby grunted with little enthusiasm.

Bo had to give him the snack or Dolby wouldn't trust him. Bo didn't think he'd earned it, though. "That was not a good woof, Dolby," he scolded.

"He's not hungry, Bo." Alice laughed. Then she concentrated on painting half a fingernail red and half blue.

"He's always hungry. Dolby, don't you want to make us famous?"

Dolby thumped his tail a couple of times. He put his chin back on his paws.

Bo patted him on the head. "Do you think he's sick, Alice?"

"I think he's *too* smart. He's suspicious of why you're feeding him again so soon after breakfast. You'll have to wait until later or catch him off guard."

"Can I—"

"No. You can't take my tape recorder outside, or to Alvin's, or anyplace." With an unpainted finger, Alice switched the machine to her favorite station.

"I'll wait until he's hungry again," Bo said. He returned most of the Woofies Snacks to the box, saving a few in his pocket for possible dog emergencies. He grabbed his pirate hat and sword and ran outside. Dolby followed reluctantly. He was sleepy, but he didn't want to miss anything.

Bo swished his sword back and forth a few times. "I'm going to see if Alvin can play," he yelled to Alice.

Bo found Alvin just finishing his breakfast. "Alvin, you and Bo play here this morning," Mrs. Stenboom said. "Bo, call your mother so she'll know where you are."

"Alice is baby-sitting," Bo explained.

"Then call Alice. She'll worry." Mrs. Stenboom shook her head and disappeared.

Bo knew Alice wouldn't worry, but he called anyway.

"Hello. You have reached 488-4871. None of the Dibbs family can come to the phone right now, but please leave a message at the sound of the beep."

Bo had forgotten that the answering machine was on. Just for fun, he dialed again and let Alvin and Dolby listen while he waited to leave his message. He figured Alice was probably sitting right there in the kitchen listening. She'd pick up the phone when she heard it was Bo.

19

When Dolby heard Mrs. Dibbs's voice coming from the receiver, his ears perked up. Before Bo could say anything, Dolby spoke for him.

"Woof-woof," he barked. *"Woof-woof-woof."*

"Did you hear that!" Bo grinned and pretended to fall over.

"Sure. Dolby barked," Alvin said. "What's so great about that? Dolby barks a lot."

"That's what I mean," Bo explained. "I've been trying to get him to bark all morning. I have to record his voice for the Woof-Off. I'll tell you all about it in a minute."

Hanging up, Bo dialed his number again. He didn't know why Alice didn't answer, but he could guess. She was in her room with the door shut and the radio on loud. It was her third favorite thing to do after talking on the phone and polishing her nails.

"Hello, you have reached—" Mrs. Dibbs's voice came on again. As if on cue, Dolby barked once more.

"Good dog," Bo praised, hugging Dolby. "Good dog."

Dolby thought this was a great game, and he loved the attention from Bo and Alvin. Bo dialed at least ten times, letting Dolby speak to the answering machine.

"I want to be sure we get a long-enough tape," Bo explained.

"Did he wait for the beep?" asked Alvin.

"I don't know." Bo was suddenly worried. "Listen for the beep, Dolby, the beep." Bo made a beeping sound several times to give Dolby the idea. "You dial, Alvin. We'd better do one or two more."

Bo and Alvin listened while Bo tried to hold Dolby's mouth shut during Mrs. Dibbs's message. Now that Bo didn't want him to bark, Dolby barked even more. *"Woof-woof. Woof-woof-woof-woof. Woof-woof."*

"That's great, Dolby," said Bo when they finished the last call. "This should be a great tape. Alice is going to be surprised."

"What is going on here?" Mrs. Stenboom came back into the kitchen. "Would you please take that dog outside, Bo. What's wrong with him?"

"He's barking," said Alvin.

"I know he's barking. Did you call Alice, Bo?"

"Sort of. But now can we go back to my house, Mrs. Stenboom, please?" Bo asked. "Alvin and I have something very important to do."

"Oh, all right. But don't give Alice a hard time."

"We won't," Bo promised.

On the way to Bo's house, the boys stopped to get Gary. By then, they were hungry, so when Mrs. Gravenstein offered them sweet rolls and milk, they couldn't say no. Finally, they fought with their swords all the way back to Bo's, arriving just as Mrs. Dibbs was pulling into the driveway.

"Oh, no." Bo looked at Alvin.

"Think she'll be mad?" Alvin asked.

"My mom would be." Gary grinned. The boys had told Gary about the contest and their phone calls while they were eating their rolls.

"Hi, boys." Mrs. Dibbs greeted them with a smile. "I can't believe I finished my errands. The traffic is awful."

Silently, the three boys and Dolby followed her into the kitchen. Mrs. Dibbs saw the answering machine's red light and pushed the REWIND button.

Ollie was in the kitchen, too, looking in the refrigerator. Rebecca had come over, and they were getting ready to work on the play.

"Can Rebecca stay for lunch?" Ollie asked.

"I guess so." Mrs. Dibbs waited for the REWIND button to stop. "My, we got a lot of calls this morning. Good thing I left the machine on."

Bo, Alvin, and Gary looked at one another. Alvin punched Bo. Bo crossed his fingers for good luck.

Pushing PLAYBACK, Mrs. Dibbs reached for the tea-kettle and filled it with water. Her face registered disbelief as the machine started to play.

"Woof-woof-woof-woof. Woof-woof-woof-woof."

"Hey, that's neat, Mrs. Dibbs," Rebecca said. "All your messages are from Dolby."

3

Bo's Great Idea

"Bo—"

"I can explain, Mom. I really can. See, Dolby wouldn't woof for Alice's recorder and then we discovered—"

"Never mind." Mrs. Dibbs slumped into a chair at the kitchen table. "Never mind."

"What's going on?" Alice sauntered into the kitchen, which seemed a popular place all of a sudden.

"It's a Woof-Off rehearsal," said Ollie, laughing.

"Where were you, Alice?" asked Mrs. Dibbs. "Why didn't you answer the phone?"

"I thought you left the machine on. My friends have my new phone number. Did I get a call here?"

"Only if you were expecting a call from Dolby." Ollie laughed again, and Rebecca joined in.

Mrs. Dibbs ignored them. "Alice, will you go get your recorder and a blank tape?" She turned to Bo.

"Bo, you tied up the phone for a long time. Your father or I might have gotten an important call."

"I won't ever have to do it again, Mom, honest I won't," Bo promised. "Besides, we have the recording now, and it's great. I just know Dolby will win. He's never woofed so much before."

"I guess I'd have to agree with that." Mrs. Dibbs got up and poured hot water over a tea bag. "Listen, maybe it would be better if we didn't mention this to your father."

"Good idea," Bo agreed.

"Make two tapes, Bo," Ollie suggested. "One could get lost in the mail."

"Yeah. We might want the sound effects for a play sometime, too," Rebecca suggested.

During lunch—Mrs. Dibbs made spaghetti and included Alvin, Gary, and Rebecca—Bo and Alice transferred the telephone tape to two blank tapes. Then Mrs. Dibbs erased the answering-machine messages from Dolby. Ollie helped Bo wrap and address the photograph of Dolby and the tape so they could get it in the box before Mr. Marzano, the Dibbses' mail carrier, came by.

Bo was just in time. No sooner had he reached the curb than he saw Mr. Marzano coming. The carrier pulled up in his jeep.

"Waiting for something important?" Mr. Marzano asked, taking the package from Bo.

"Not yet," Bo answered. "It will take at least a week to hear back." Bo explained about the Woof-Off contest.

"Dolby's going to be a finalist; I know he will. He's got the best dog voice in the Rocky Mountains. Maybe even in the country."

"Is that so?" Mr. Marzano handed Bo the Dibbses' mail.

Dolby woofed to prove it.

"Dolby certainly sounds confident," the young mail carrier said. "Good luck."

On Saturday afternoon, Bo taught Dolby to cry. Bo would look very sad and cry loudly. Dolby would perk up his ears, paw at Bo, and whine. Bo would then reward him with a Woofies Snack. He also used the word *cry* every time they did the trick.

"I read about a dog that knew a hundred words," Ollie said, stopping to watch Bo and Dolby begin to work on *fetch*. "But that probably meant both commands and words like *food* and *water* and *car*."

"Yeah, maybe stuff like *chocolate* and *peanut butter* and *steak*." Bo looked at Dolby to see whether he reacted to any of those words. Dolby thumped his tail, ready to play some more. "Sit," Bo said. "Stay."

He took a ball from the side yard into the back and left it where the big dog could see it. Dolby sat and watched with a wiggle of anticipation. Then Bo walked slowly all the way back to Dolby. "Fetch," Bo called. Dolby raced away, grabbed the ball, and was back in seconds.

On the third *fetch*, Dolby stopped in his tracks, looking at something in the grass. Bo and Ollie went to see what Dolby had found.

"It's just a garter snake," said Ollie. "Maybe Dolby is tired of fetching and wants to watch the snake."

"He can't get tired so easily if he's going to practice enough to win," complained Bo. "But I guess there won't be any snakes to worry about in the gym during the contest."

"Probably not," agreed Ollie.

"I'm going to make a list of words he knows," Bo said. He had learned to make lists from Ollie. Ollie made lists every time he needed to think about something or make a decision. Bo sat at the picnic table as he thought and wrote and wrote and thought.

By Sunday morning, Bo realized he needed to teach Dolby many more tricks and a lot more words. After the judges liked Dolby's woof, they'd want to see how smart he was. With less than five weeks until the finals, he and Dolby faced a lot of work. Bo knew it took time and patience to train a dog well. But it was going to be worth it. Bo took a deep breath. Many a time, Ollie had said to him, "Success doesn't come easily. The people that work hardest are the most successful."

"The dog that works hardest is going to win," Bo told the big dog. Dolby liked Bo playing with him so much, he was willing to cooperate.

Putting the training wheels back on his bicycle—he'd outgrown them long ago, but the Dibbses saved or recycled almost everything—Bo tried to get Dolby to ride it. He'd seen animals in the circus riding bikes.

"Get on the bike," Bo said to Dolby, pointing to the seat. He tried to lift one of Dolby's front feet onto the pedal. Finally, Dolby stood, leaning on the bike seat, but he couldn't get on it. Bo wasn't strong enough to lift him. "Maybe we need a box." He ran into the garage and pulled out a medium-sized cardboard box that books had come in. It was strong enough to hold Dolby, but even when Dolby got up on the box and sat, he couldn't step onto the bike.

While Bo thought about what to do, he found a party hat and put it on Dolby. It had an elastic string to hold it on. Dolby looked really funny, and Bo nearly fell over laughing. Dolby hung his head.

Frustrated that Dolby couldn't get on the bike, Bo put his hands on his hips and said, "Try again, Dolby. Jump. You have to learn some new tricks. You could get up there if you tried harder. Bad dog, Dolby. Bad dog."

About that time, Ollie came along. "Dolby isn't bad, Bo. He's embarrassed. Can't you see that? Animal trainers have to be sensitive to what an animal is thinking."

"Embarrassed? Dolby is embarrassed?" asked Bo.

"Sure. Animals don't like to look foolish or be laughed at. You've made Dolby look foolish. I realize now that Dolby was probably embarrassed that time we made him pretend to be a tiger, but I didn't know it then. He's such a good dog, sometimes I think he pretends just to please us."

When Oliver was collecting for the Save-the-Tiger

fund, he and Bo had painted non-toxic orange and white stripes on Dolby. They hung a sign on his back and took him to the mall. People did think they were cute and donated a lot of money, but the boys ended up in trouble over it. Now Ollie tried to think everything out before he acted on what seemed like good ideas.

"I would never have thought of that, Ollie," said Bo, taking the hat off Dolby. "I wish you'd help me. This is hard work." He sat down, looking discouraged.

"I just don't have time, Bo," Ollie said. "Rebecca is coming over and we're going to Frank's house. Frank doesn't have as much time now for our play. He entered his collie, Basher, in the Woof-Off, too."

"I hope Basher doesn't mind losing to Dolby," Bo said.

After lunch, Alice greased herself to lie in the sun on the patio and get a suntan. It was a very warm day for April. She thought suntans were romantic.

"Are you going to be here for about an hour, Alice?" Mrs. Dibbs asked. She and Mr. Dibbs came outside dressed in shorts. "Ollie is going to Frank's. Your father and I want to play tennis. Will you watch Bo?"

"Why can't he go with Ollie?" Alice asked, flopping on a lawn chair and adjusting her sunglasses.

"I don't want to, Alice," Bo said. "I need to teach Dolby more tricks." Bo didn't mention that Ollie probably didn't want him tagging along. "Besides, Alvin spent the night with his grandmother in Denver while his parents went to a play. He's going to call me as soon as they get back. Are you going to leave the machine on, Dad? I can answer the phone."

"No, my team is all set and ready for Mexico. I don't want anyone to mention work today. And maybe we'll do something special as a family later on."

"All right," Alice agreed. "I'll watch Bo." She got up and spread her beach towel on the chair. Then she arranged her new magazine on the patio floor, even with the head of the chair, so she could read it while lying on her stomach.

Everyone else left. Bo sat on the back step watching Alice fry herself. Dolby sat with Bo for a few minutes. Then he trotted off to the shade of the big cottonwoods in the Dibbses' backyard. When the phone rang, Bo ran to answer.

The call was from a man selling subscriptions to the *Daily Camera,* Boulder's newspaper. "We already get it," said Bo. "Lester Philpott throws it in our driveway every morning." Lester was a bully who had given Bo and Ollie a lot of trouble in the past.

Finally, Bo got tired of waiting for Alvin to call. He moved to the shade to help Dolby watch another garter snake.

He was so fascinated with the snake, he forgot about Dolby. Suddenly, he heard the big dog barking. Swinging around, he could see that Alice was gone. Dolby was standing by the open back door.

The phone, he thought. Dolby often barked when it rang. Bo leaped up and dashed toward the house. He got there just in time. "Hello," he struggled to say, out of breath.

It was Alvin. "Hey, Bo. I was about to hang up. I'm home. Can you come over now?"

"No. Alice is watching me while everyone else is gone. You come over here."

"Okay. Be there in five minutes," Alvin said.

Bo hung up the phone. Alice was no place in sight, but her radio was still blaring on the patio. It was a wonder Dolby had heard the phone ringing.

"Thanks, Dolby. Good thing you were paying attention. Why didn't you just answer the phone?" Bo laughed at his joke.

The more he thought about it, though, the better it sounded. Why couldn't Dolby answer the phone? He often barked when it rang, anyway.

What a great idea! Bo slammed his fist against the palm of his hand. He'd teach Dolby to answer the phone. Dolby could lift off the receiver, put it down, woof *"Wait a minute,"* then go and get Bo. At the contest for the finalists, Dolby could do the trick for the judges. Bo bet that no other dog in the contest would be able to answer the telephone.

Bo thought it would be great if Dolby answered the call saying he had been selected for the Woof-Off final. He jumped up and down, laughing at his best idea yet.

4

Dolby's Best Trick

Teaching Dolby to answer the phone proved to be more difficult than Bo had thought, until Alvin remembered his little sister's toy phone. He ran home to get it.

The two boys sat in the backyard in the shade and practiced. Alvin would ring the bell on the toy phone. Bo would pick up the receiver, hold it out to Dolby, and say, "Answer, Dolby, answer. Speak, Dolby, speak."

Dolby watched the boys patiently, thumping his tail on the grass. When the bell on the toy phone jingled, he'd perk up his ears, but otherwise he just watched. Sometimes he would woof when Bo said, "Speak," but he was tired of that game, too.

Finally, Dolby stretched full length under a tree and fell asleep. Bo was ready to give up. Maybe the trick was too hard for Dolby. Then he had another idea. Dolby was extremely fond of candy. He especially liked the kind that mixed chocolate and peanut butter. He wasn't allowed to have much, but Bo decided this was a very important occasion.

"Keep Dolby here, Alvin," Bo said, jumping up.

"That's easy," Alvin said. He leaned back against the tree himself, pretending to doze.

Bo knew where his mother kept her emergency supply of candy bars. He dug into the back of the cupboard. What luck. There was one peanut-butter cup left. Dolby would eat a Milky Way or a Baby Ruth—he wouldn't eat coconut—but he preferred peanut butter. Bo grabbed some Woofies treats, too, figuring he'd better mix the two rewards. In the contest, of course, he'd only reward Dolby with Woofies, since they were the sponsor of the event.

"I'm not supposed to give him candy," said Bo, running back to where Alvin and Dolby dozed. "But I figure this is an emergency."

"Yeah, I'd say so," Alvin agreed.

There was something about the crackling of a candy wrapper that always caught Dolby's attention. He sat up, ears alert, turning his head sideways. He wiggled and whined a little in anticipation of a possible treat.

"Oh, I think I'll have a *chocolate* and *peanut-butter cup*," Bo said in a loud, teasing voice. "I'm sure Dolby won't want any. It's working, Alvin," he whispered from behind one hand.

Carefully, Bo took the peanut-butter cup and smeared some of it over the receiver of the toy telephone. The afternoon heat already was making the candy soft. He licked the extra off his fingers before he started the trick.

"Now ring the bell, Alvin." Bo held the receiver between two fingers.

Brrring, brrring. The toy bell jingled.

"Answer the phone, Dolby," Bo said. "Answer the *phone*." He said the key word louder and handed the receiver to Dolby.

Of course, Dolby took the receiver in his mouth, slobbering on Bo's fingers in the process.

"Good dog, Dolby, good dog," praised Bo. He tossed Dolby a Woofies Doggie Snack iced with just a bit of chocolate.

The boys repeated the trick over and over. After the third time, and for all the rest, Bo put the candy underneath and left the receiver on the phone. Then Dolby had to lift it off to lick the peanut butter and chocolate. Excessive praise and the treats worked. Soon, when the bell jangled, Dolby lifted the receiver off the phone even when there was no candy smeared on it.

Then Bo made the trick harder. After Dolby answered the phone, Bo commanded him to speak. Soon Dolby got that idea, too.

"Now for the final test," said Bo, very proud of Dolby. "You run home, Alvin. Call Dolby and tell him to speak when he answers the phone."

Alvin scrambled up and ran to his house. Bo and Dolby casually sauntered past Alice, who had returned to her suntanning and magazine.

"What are you up to, Bo?" she asked.

"What makes you think I'm up to something, Alice?" Bo pretended to be mad.

"You usually are." Alice turned over, moved her sunglasses from the top of her head onto her nose, and put more oil on her arms and legs.

Inside, Bo quietly pushed the back door so that it was almost closed. He turned the telephone to SOFT RING. He smeared a little bit of chocolate from the candy wrapper onto the receiver. Then he and Dolby sat down on the kitchen floor to wait. Bo crossed his fingers, hoping that the trick would work with the real phone and that Alice wouldn't run in to answer when it rang. With any luck, she wouldn't even hear it with her radio on.

Brrring, brrring. In about five minutes, the phone shrilled quietly. Dolby had no trouble hearing it. His ears were sensitive to shrill noises. First, he sat up straighter. He looked at the wall phone, but Bo didn't think that its position should make a difference.

"Answer the phone, Dolby. Answer the *phone*," Bo whispered in the big dog's ear. "Chocolate, Dolby, *chocolate*. Answer the phone. *Peanut butter*. Answer the phone."

Chocolate and *peanut butter* might or might not have been in Dolby's vocabulary, but *phone* was. The boys had done a good job of teaching him that. He walked over to the counter and looked up.

Keep ringing, Alvin, keep ringing, Bo thought. He'd forgotten to tell Alvin it might take time for Dolby to connect the toy phone with the real phone. "Answer the phone, Dolby. Good dog. Answer the phone."

Dolby stood up, placing his paws on the side of the counter. He smelled the candy on the phone receiver. Slowly, carefully, he opened his mouth, lifted the receiver, placed it on the floor, and licked it.

"Speak, Dolby, speak," said Alvin.

Dolby cocked his head, hearing Alvin's voice.

"Speak, Dolby, speak," Alvin repeated.

"Woof-woof," barked Dolby into the phone. *"Woof-woof."*

"Good dog, Dolby, good dog," shouted Alvin.

Bo fell over laughing. He was too happy to praise Dolby. It worked! His trick had worked!

"Call again, Alvin," said Bo when he could finally stop laughing. "We have to do it several times now while he remembers."

Fortunately, Mr. and Mrs. Dibbs didn't return until Dolby had successfully answered the phone five times.

Mrs. Dibbs collapsed in a chair at the kitchen table. "Boy, did I get out of shape this winter," she said, fanning herself with a magazine.

"Did I get any calls, Bo?" asked Mr. Dibbs, heading for the refrigerator to get two glasses of iced tea.

"No, Dad," Bo said. "All the calls were for me or Alice." Or Dolby, he thought, smiling.

5

Alice Protests

"You aren't still worried about people seeing your patch, are you, Bo?" Mr. Dibbs watched his son staring at his breakfast cereal.

All weekend, Bo had been too busy to think much about going to school wearing the eye patch. Now that it was Monday, he did worry. "Some, Dad." He moved his soggy flakes from one side of the bowl to the other. "But I guess I'll just explain about my lazy eye."

"People usually don't laugh about things once they understand them," Mr. Dibbs said. "That would be the best approach to take. Maybe Mrs. Henderson will let you tell the whole class."

"Yeah, I'll go in early and talk to her." That way, thought Bo, no one would see him on the playground before school, either.

That was exactly the plan that Mrs. Henderson suggested after Bo finished explaining about his eye. "You can share your eye patch during show-and-tell, Bo. Will you have to wear glasses?" she asked.

"I might," Bo said. "Ollie wears glasses. Maybe it runs in the family." Having good ideas must run in the Dibbs family, too, Bo thought, but he kept the notion to himself. He wasn't ready to tell Mrs. Henderson that Dolby could answer the telephone.

He had wanted to show Ollie but hadn't had the chance. Ollie was going to be both surprised and proud. He'd probably say, "Wow, Bo, you have good ideas just like I do. Dolby is sure to win the contest."

Thinking how impressed Ollie would be helped Bo stand a little taller as his class came in and stared at him. Sheri Longholtz stared, too, but she also smiled. Bo hoped they'd have show-and-tell right away.

They did, and Mrs. Henderson asked Bo to explain his eye patch. He did, quickly, but then he didn't sit down.

"I have something better to tell about than my eye." Bo grinned at the class.

"What's that, Bo?" Mrs. Henderson never made people hurry their show-and-tell sharing.

"I'm entering my dog, Dolby, in a contest called a Woof-Off. When he wins, he's going to make dog-food commercials for TV. Then he and I both are going to be famous."

"How do you know he's going to win?" asked Chester Charlton.

"Yeah, some other dog might be better," said Brittany Wyatt.

Before Bo could say anything, Mrs. Henderson interrupted. "What does being famous mean to you, Bo?"

What did it mean? Everybody knew what being famous meant. Bo tried to put his feelings into words. "Well . . . it means being rich and everyone knows your name and . . . and . . ."

Mrs. Henderson smiled at Bo. "What does everyone else think?" she asked.

"It might not be so great," Lucy Hodges said, standing up so everyone could see her new dress. "When you're famous, everyone wants your autograph. My sister collects autographs of rock stars. She has two so far. If you're famous and go shopping, everyone will want your autograph. You won't have any time left to try on clothes."

Bo didn't do much shopping for clothes—certainly not as much as Lucy Hodges and her sister, Brenda, who was in Ollie's class. He didn't think that would be any problem.

"If a new person wanted to be your friend," said Sam Satori, "you wouldn't know if he really liked you or wanted to be friends because you were famous. My brother said everyone wanted to be his friend when he made the winning touchdown in the homecoming football game." Bo knew that Sam had a lot of friends. He probably wasn't worried about making new ones.

Bo knew Alvin and Gary would always be his best friends, no matter how famous he got.

"When you went out to eat, your Big Mac and fries would get cold and soggy because people would want to talk to you," said Jimbo Wilson. Jimbo was the biggest first grader in the school. He never let a hamburger get cold or ice cream melt before he ate it.

"My brother, Ollie, is famous, and he has plenty of time left over for projects." Bo was ready to sit down. He didn't much like this discussion. "Anyway, I didn't mean I'd be as famous as George Washington or Michael Jackson."

"Let's all write some sentences about being famous," suggested Mrs. Henderson. "Start this way." She went to the board and printed "If I was famous, I'd . . ."

Bo sat down. He got out his pencil and took the writing paper that Sheri passed out. Holding the pencil tightly, he wrote all he could think of: "If I was famous, I'd be happy." Some people had suggested that being famous would be bad, but he knew better.

At first recess, even though he'd explained about his patch, kids teased Bo.

"Maybe you can become a famous pirate, Bo," said Jimbo. "Pirates are rich, too."

"And you wouldn't have to sign autographs," pointed out Sam Satori, "because you'd be at sea on your pirate ship."

"Don't pay any attention to them, Bo," said Sheri, who walked beside him. "I think you look cute wearing that patch. What's in the bag?"

Bo didn't want Sheri to say he looked cute, but he was pleased she didn't laugh. Jimbo almost had spoiled the surprise Bo was planning. "You'll see," answered Bo.

He looked for Alvin and Gary, who'd had to stay and talk to Mrs. Henderson about giggling during silent-reading period. If she hadn't moved Bo into the front row so he could see the board, he probably would have been in trouble, too.

Finally, Alvin and Gary came running toward him with their grocery bags. As soon as they set them down, the three boys opened their bags together and pulled out the pirate hats.

"Ta-dah," Bo said to Sheri, who kept hanging around him.

The boys hadn't brought their swords, knowing Mrs. Henderson would take them away. They fought as best they could with invisible ones. Neither Gary nor Alvin had his eye patch, either.

"Where are your eye patches?" asked Bo.

"My mother says I can't keep wearing my patch, Bo," said Gary. "She said it might do the opposite of what your patch is supposed to do."

"That's all right," said Bo. "I'm getting used to this."

"I was telling Gary about you know what," Alvin said, pretending to be talking on the phone. "Can we show him Dolby's trick after school, Bo?"

Bo forgot the teasing. He forgot about playing pirate, or even becoming a famous pirate, which wasn't a totally bad idea.

"Sure. We need to do it a lot or he'll forget it, and besides, I want to show Ollie."

"What can Dolby do?" asked Sheri.

"Nothing," answered Bo. "Nothing that an ordinary

genius dog couldn't learn. I'll show you, too, some-time."

That afternoon, Alice had two friends visiting. They raided the refrigerator for Cokes and made popcorn, then disappeared into Alice's room and shut the door. It was a perfect time for Bo and Dolby to show off.

Gary and Ollie waited expectantly in the Dibbses' kitchen. Alvin had complained about being left out, but Bo reminded him that someone had to telephone.

Dolby hadn't had such an audience in a long time, so he was eager to show off. He did exactly what Bo expected of him, what they had worked a long time to perfect. When the phone rang, he answered it.

"Speak, Dolby, speak," Alvin said.

Dolby woofed on cue and everyone in the kitchen screamed with laughter.

"That's great, Bo!" Ollie said. "That's a super trick."

Bo tingled all over at Ollie's praise. At last, he'd thought of something neat to do all by himself.

Then Ollie got on the phone and called Rebecca and Frank, first wiping the receiver on his jeans. "Ugh, dog spit," he said.

Bo and Gary laughed. "Dog spit, dog spit," they repeated, giggling.

Ollie persuaded Alvin to stay home and call one more time after Rebecca and Frank got to the Dibbses' house. He did, and Rebecca and Frank thought it was the best trick they had ever seen a dog perform.

"Are you going to have him do that at the Woof-

Off?" asked Frank. "If you do, he may beat out my collie, Basher, for sure."

"I'll have to think about it," answered Bo, pleased about the attention that Ollie's friends were giving him. "No fair teaching Basher this trick, though."

"He could never do that," Frank assured him. "In fact, he won't do many tricks. I'm going to have to rely on his looks."

"What if Dolby doesn't get accepted for the regional contest, Bo?" Rebecca asked. "You and Frank seem to be sure both dogs are in."

Bo didn't want to think about Dolby not being a finalist. "I know he will, Rebecca. You heard the tape."

"And Basher's the best-looking dog in town," added Frank. "His photo was fantastic."

Ollie decided to make popcorn for them all. "This is to celebrate Dolby's success," he said. Alvin had just come in when the telephone surprised them by ringing again. They looked at each other. Then Ollie grabbed the phone before Dolby could answer.

"Ollie?" It was Mrs. Dibbs. "Is everything okay there?"

"Sure, Mom. We're fine," Ollie said. "Is it all right if I make popcorn? Rebecca and Frank are here." Ollie didn't mention Alvin and Gary.

"Yes. Where's Alice?"

"She's in her room. Do you want to talk to her?"

"No. I was just checking in." Mrs. Dibbs often called to check on the boys, probably knowing Alice wasn't always paying attention to them. She was there for emergencies, though, and Ollie was very reliable. "I've been testing these computers all day, Ollie, and I'm exhausted. I don't even want to have to push any buttons on the microwave. How about pizza for dinner? I can stop and get it on the way home."

"Great, Mom. Get one pepperoni, and I'll make a salad," Ollie said, then hung up. "Whew, that was close. I doubt if Mom would want Dolby answering the phone all the time."

Everyone agreed, then collapsed into laughter at the idea. Alice and her friends came into the kitchen and looked at the crowd. "What's going on? I don't think Mother would want all of you over here when I'm baby-sitting. I'm not being paid to hostess a party."

"It's not a party, Alice," Bo answered. "It's a Woof-Off."

"Good grief." Alice looked at her friends as if to say, Why me? "At least take that popcorn outside. I'll make you some lemonade."

Bo, Ollie, and their friends took their popcorn outside and settled around the picnic table. While Alice's friends set up lawn chairs, Alice poured lemonade for everyone. Ollie was telling the younger boys about collecting money for the Denver Zoo's new Reptile House when the phone rang.

"That's *him*," screamed Roberta Singer.

"Yeah!" Audrey Nichols jumped up and down, shrieking. "Roberta gave him your family's phone number, Alice. You want to be sure you like him before you give him your private number."

"Don't you dare answer it," Alice shouted. "It's for me." She started running toward the kitchen.

When Alice yelled at them, Bo, Ollie, and their friends froze. But Dolby, who had been sitting near the picnic table waiting for popcorn, thought the game had begun again.

He dashed for the open back door. Knowing what was going to happen, Bo, Ollie, and their friends jumped up and followed. Alice's friends were right behind her, but Dolby had a head start on everyone. In seconds, Dolby was in the kitchen, paws on the counter, the receiver in his mouth. Laying the phone on the floor carefully, he spoke without anyone having to prompt him.

"Woof-woof," he said. *"Wait a minute. Woof-woof."*

Alice stopped dead in her tracks the minute she entered the kitchen. Bo covered his other eye and scrunched his shoulders. Ollie looked at Rebecca and Frank and grinned. Alvin and Gary covered their mouths and giggled.

"I may get killed," whispered Bo.

There was a tense silence, then Alice carefully picked up the phone between two fingers. "Hello," she said, her voice like the calm before a storm. "Yes, it is. Could you please call me back in five minutes at another number?" Alice repeated her private phone number. "We have an emergency here. Yes, thank you." She placed the receiver back on the hook.

Bo looked at Ollie and bit his bottom lip.

Alice stiffened her arms and made her hands into fists. "Bo? Ollie? That's gross! Who taught Dolby to answer the phone? That was my new friend, Hamilton Byers the Third. I have never been so embarrassed in my whole life," she shrieked. "What is he going to think of me, living in a house where a dog answers the phone? He'll never call me back. Mom and Dad are going to hear about this as soon as they get home. Someone is going to get killed!"

"What harm can a little trick do, Alice?" Bo said, protesting weakly as Alice stopped for breath. "It was really hard to teach Dolby that, and he's going to do it in the Woof-Off contest."

"Yeah, Alice," Ollie added. "It's a neat trick. You should be proud to live in a family with such a smart dog. Please don't tell Mom and Dad."

"They won't care," Bo added, afraid they would. He was pleased that Ollie had stuck up for him and Dolby, though.

"They will so care. And anything could go wrong. Mom and Dad both get business calls at home."

"It is kind of cute," Roberta said.

"Yeah, it must have been hard to teach him that." Audrey smiled at Bo.

"I'll watch Dolby, Alice," Bo pleaded. "I promise I will. I won't let him answer business calls."

"How would you know if a call's about business or not?" Alice had the last word. She stood looking at both boys for a minute. Then she harrumphed and motioned to her friends. Quickly, the three of them ran upstairs to Alice's room and closed the door.

"Think she'll tell?" Bo asked Ollie.

"Maybe not," Ollie said. "But you'd better keep your eye on Dolby."

"I will," Bo promised, starting to breathe normally again. "I sure will."

6

Good Progress

By the next Friday, lots of people in Bo's and Ollie's classes had heard about Dolby's trick. Of course, they called, wanting to hear Dolby answer the phone. Fortunately, it was right after school when Bo or Ollie was there to talk to them. Alice hardly ever answered the family phone, knowing her own friends would call on her private line.

Friday afternoon, Dolby met Bo and Ollie just as they were coming up the driveway.

"*Woof-woof. Woof-woof,*" Dolby barked.

Bo ran to the back door, which stood open. Apparently, Alice had just gotten home and hadn't bothered to close it. Dolby could open the screen. The first thing Alice usually did was turn off the answering machine on the phone so Bo and Ollie could get calls from their friends. Mr. and Mrs. Dibbs had said that was all right. They wanted to be able to check on the kids, too, or

51

give them instructions about starting dinner. Bo considered it a miracle that Dolby hadn't answered a call from his mom or dad. Since both Ollie and Bo knew their parents most often called after four, they took over from Dolby then.

Alice knew about kids calling to hear Dolby bark. Once she'd gotten over being mad, she was a good sport about keeping the trick a secret. Bo had seen her wipe off the receiver a couple of times before their parents got home. Now the phone receiver lay on the kitchen floor.

"I hope it's for me," Bo said, picking up the phone. "Maybe it's the call saying Dolby is a finalist. Hello."

"Hi, Bo." It was Lester Philpott. Bo never had talked to Lester on the phone, but there was no doubt it was Lester's voice. "I just wanted to see if what I heard was true—that Dolby could answer the phone. That's a neat trick. I told him to go get you and he did."

There was admiration in Lester's voice, but Bo didn't trust it. Ollie and Lester were in the same class at school. Even though Lester could be really mean, Ollie had given him an important role in their class campaign to elect stegosaurus state fossil. Ollie claimed that Lester had been a nicer person ever since, but that didn't mean he was a friend of Bo's.

"Could I see him do it if I come over?" Lester asked.

Bo covered the phone with his hand and whispered to Ollie. "Lester wants to come see Dolby answer the phone."

"Well . . ." Ollie thought a second. He really didn't

trust Lester, either. "I guess it would be all right. Why not? We should try to be friends with Lester. He needs friends. Get Alvin to call."

"All right, Lester," Bo told him. "You can come over for a few minutes. Then I have work to do. I have to train Dolby every day for the Woof-Off."

Bo and Ollie searched for something to eat. Dolby sat in the middle of the kitchen looking proud of himself.

"Good dog, Dolby," Bo said. "Good dog." He tossed Dolby two Woofies Snacks.

"Who was that on the phone, Bo?" Alice came into the kitchen. "I was in the bathroom. Did Dolby answer it? What are you going to do when Mom or Dad calls and Dolby answers?"

Bo didn't answer the last two questions. "It was Lester Philpott, Alice."

"Lester Philpott? What did he want?"

"He wants to see Dolby answer the phone," Bo admitted.

"Good grief." Alice sighed and looked in the refrigerator. "I hope Lester isn't going to start hanging around here, too."

"He isn't, Alice," Ollie assured her. "He has stopped bullying me now, but I don't want to spend a lot of time with him."

"Do either of you have homework?" Alice asked.

"I don't," said Bo.

"Me, either," answered Ollie. "I'm going up to my room to read about snakes. I also need to think up one more activity to raise money. We've almost reached our goal for collecting money for the zoo's Reptile House, but I'd like to go over it."

Alice took her glass of milk and a piece of cake and disappeared. Ollie did the same. That left Bo to deal with Lester. To Bo's surprise, Lester acted really friendly. Bo called Alvin and asked him to call the Dibbses' phone number. Sure enough, Dolby performed perfectly.

A big grin spread over Lester's face. "That's really neat, Bo. It's the funniest thing I've ever seen a dog do. Dolby's pretty smart, isn't he? You think he'll win the Woof-Off?"

Lester seemed to know a lot about Bo's business, Bo thought. "I have to train him to do more tricks, Lester. I'm sure he'll win, though."

"I sure hope so, Bo. I'd like to know a famous dog."

As they went back outside onto the patio, Bo called, "Fetch," and threw Dolby's tennis ball. Dolby dashed off across the yard. In seconds, he was back without the ball but with a present for Bo, a thank-you gift for being such a great pal.

"Dolby!" Bo cried. "Don't eat that snake!" Because it was small, Dolby had the snake all the way in his mouth.

"He's not eating it," Lester pointed out. He took the snake out of Dolby's mouth. "He's part retriever, isn't he? Retrievers have soft mouths. That means they know how to pick up ducks and stuff like that without biting into them. See? This snake isn't one bit hurt."

Lester held up the garter snake, which wiggled and wrapped itself around Lester's fingers. He handed it to Bo for inspection.

"I guess it isn't." Bo looked the snake over carefully, running his fingers over its cool, smooth skin. He watched it flick its tongue in and out. Snakes are neat, he thought. Now he needed to get down to the business at hand, training Dolby. He didn't want to invite Lester to stay and watch.

"I guess I'd better go," Lester said finally. "See you."

"Sure, Lester. Bye." Bo breathed a sigh of relief. He fetched a pocketful of Woofies Snacks and a bandanna and took Dolby into the backyard.

Bo had made a list of things to work on for his and Dolby's program. It could last five to ten minutes, but Bo figured five would be long enough.

His list read:

Roll over. (Make this trick perfect.)
Play dead.
Fetch.
Cry. (Handkerchief.)

Bo had had to ask Ollie twice how to spell *handkerchief*. Dolby knew the word *cry*. *Handkerchief* would be a new word for him today. Bo was actually going to use a bandanna, since it was larger, but he'd call it a handkerchief.

"Roll over." Bo started with the easiest trick.

Dolby lay down and flipped over. Then he decided his back was itchy, so he rolled back and forth several times, wiggling, his long legs in the air.

"Play dead," called Bo. "*Dead,*" he said, raising his voice.

Dolby wasn't in the mood to die, but finally he lay still. Then he opened one eye to see if it was time to come back to life.

"Good dog, Dolby. Good dog." Bo tossed the Woofies, then patted Dolby on the head. He had a great idea.

"Play dead, Dolby. Dead." Dolby did as he was told. Then Bo sat down and started to cry because Dolby had died. He didn't know whether he'd use this in the program, but he wanted to see what would happen. Dolby came back to life, raised his ears, cocked his head, and whined. Finally, he pushed his nose into Bo's face.

"Good dog, Dolby, good dog!" Bo gave him two Woofies. This was great. Dolby had performed two tricks back-to-back. That was the key to a good program—one thing happening right after another. Now if Dolby would go right on to *fetch,* this would be wonderful. Bo pulled the bandanna from his back pocket.

"Hi, Bo," a voice behind him said. "How's Dolby doing?"

It was Sheri Longholtz. She was wearing tight, shiny red shorts, a top with silver trim, and was twirling a baton. She had on large sunglasses with pink rims. They were too big for her, but Bo thought she looked really cute.

"Hi, Sheri. He's doing great. Want to see the show as far as I've gotten?"

"Sure." Sheri perched on the edge of a lawn chair to watch.

When Dolby had run through his repertoire, she clapped. Then she jumped up and cheered, twirled her baton, and tossed it into the air. When it came back down, she missed catching it, and her sunglasses flew off. Bo ran to pick up the glasses.

"Oh, thanks. I'd hate to lose those. I just got them at C-Mart. Do you like them?"

"They're sure better than a patch," Bo said.

"Oh, look, isn't that cute? Dolby picked up my baton."

Sure enough, Dolby stood near Sheri, the long silver stick in his mouth.

"Good dog, Dolby, good dog," said Bo, laughing. "I'm always throwing a stick for him to fetch. I guess he thought this was his new fancy stick."

"I could use him when I'm practicing tossing. I can't catch it yet."

"You'll get better. I'm sure you will. Any trick takes a lot of work to learn. Ask Dolby."

Sheri giggled. "I know. Teaching someone to do tricks is a lot of work, too. I think you're great, Bo. You're as smart as your brother, Ollie. I know Dolby is going to win the Woof-Off. Then when he's on television, I can say I know him."

Spinning around, twirling the baton at the same time, Sheri jumped into the air. She ran across the backyard and toward home. She lived across the field, next door to Frank Ashburn and Basher.

Bo watched her go, feeling all warm inside. "She's wonderful, isn't she, Dolby? Speak if you think Sheri Longholtz is wonderful."

"*Woof-woof,*" barked Dolby. "*Woof-woof.*"

"If she's noticing me now, just think how much she'll like me when I'm famous."

"*Woof-woof. Woof-woof.*"

"Oops, sorry, Dolby. When *we're* famous."

7

Caught in the Act

"How's the Dolby training going?" Mr. Dibbs asked that night at dinner.

"He knows all his old tricks really well," answered Bo. "And I'm teaching him some new ones, but I'm sure I need to think of more."

"Oh, I don't know." Alice joined the conversation. "Probably the judges will think Dolby's so amazing, they'll declare him the winner the minute they see him. My friends think he's amazing. Hamilton thinks Dolby knows the funniest tricks he's ever heard of." She grinned at Bo.

Bo waited. Was she going to tell on him and Dolby? Alice didn't say any more, and he sighed. So far, so good, but leave it to Alice to give him a hard time. He knew he had been lucky that neither of his parents had called when Dolby was answering the phone. One day, Mrs. Dibbs had complained about the downstairs phone being so dirty, but he didn't think she suspected anything.

"Well," said Mrs. Dibbs, "if Dolby is so amazing, he can learn how to work in the yard. Your father ordered gravel to landscape a new flower bed. It'll be delivered tomorrow. If we all work together to finish the yard work, we can go for a picnic on Sunday. Would you like that?"

Alice groaned, but Ollie and Bo nodded.

"Can we go to Sawhill Ponds?" Ollie asked. "The red-wing blackbirds and the geese will be nesting. We might be able to see muskrats and beavers, since there will be lots of fish for them to catch."

"That's a good idea," Mr. Dibbs agreed.

"Do I have to go?" asked Alice. "Hamilton and I were going to play tennis."

"You're playing tennis, Alice?" Mrs. Dibbs smiled. "Great. Maybe we can play with you if you wait until afternoon."

"I thought you said you didn't like getting all sweaty." Ollie had a good memory for things Alice said.

"Playing with Hamilton is different." She made a face at Ollie. "But we aren't good enough to play with you and Dad, Mom."

"Your mother and I are going to play on the mixed-doubles tennis ladder this year," said Mr. Dibbs. "We need a lot of practice. Go with Hamilton, but I hope you'll play with us another time."

Mr. and Mrs. Dibbs were very good tennis players. They had encouraged Alice to play, but she wasn't terribly athletic. That's why her announcement came as a surprise. Ollie was so involved in his causes, he didn't want to take the time to learn a sport.

"Maybe you can start playing tennis this summer, Bo," said Mrs. Dibbs.

"I figure I'll be too busy with Dolby. We'll be doing commercials all the time. Do you think they'll make the Woofies Dog Food commercials in Boulder, or will Dolby and I have to travel all over the world?"

"Good grief," said Alice. "You're making too much of all this, Bo. Isn't he, Mom? Tell him."

"Dolby hasn't even been accepted for the regional contest, Bo," Ollie reminded his brother.

"I have to be confident, don't I, Ollie?" Bo said, a waver in his voice. "You always say you have to believe in yourself. If I don't believe in Dolby, he sure won't win." Bo couldn't understand why everyone was trying to discourage him.

"We believe in you and Dolby, Bo," said Mr. Dibbs. "But you're getting way ahead of yourself. There is such a thing as being overconfident. We don't want you to be too disappointed if all your hopes don't come true."

"I know Dolby won't let me down, will you, boy?" Bo patted Dolby's head when he stood up beside the table. "Can Dolby and I call Alvin and Gary from the upstairs phone, Dad? Can I ask them to go along to Sawhill Ponds?"

"Not my phone, Bo," Alice warned him.

"Yes, invite them," said Mrs. Dibbs. "And you can invite someone, Ollie, if you like."

Early the next morning, when the gravel was dumped in the Dibbses' driveway, everyone had to work to transfer it to the bed near the mailbox.

"Help me listen for the telephone, Bo," Mr. Dibbs said, making sure the back door stayed open. He wheeled a barrow of gravel down the driveway. "I'm expecting a very important call from a scientist in California, Dan Malcowitz. We've designed a new lens, and he's working on a business deal in California that's going to make us rich and famous. He may need to talk to me before he closes it." Mr. Dibbs laughed at the idea of getting rich.

"You can have part of Dolby's money, Dad. He'll make the whole family rich." Bo didn't tell his father that Dolby would also let them know if the phone rang.

"Do you promise?" Mr. Dibbs looked at Dolby, who was asleep in the shade of the cherry tree. "He doesn't look very ambitious."

Bo laughed, too. Dolby's legs were moving. He must be dreaming about chasing rabbits at Sawhill Ponds. Bo hadn't told him he'd have to stay on a leash.

"Well"—Bo tried not to get overconfident about the idea—"maybe not, but it's possible, don't you think?"

Once they started raking the gravel, Dolby went a little crazy. He bounced and barked and chased at the round pebbles that rolled into the driveway. When none rolled by themselves, he jumped in the pile and kicked some out.

"Dad may not like this trick," whispered Ollie as he and Bo stopped to watch Dolby.

"But he's sure funny, isn't he, Ollie?" Bo giggled.

"Bo!" Dad ordered, tiring of Dolby's game. "Put this dog in the house. He's lost his mind."

Bo caught Dolby, who was slowing down a little, anyway. "Come on, Dolby. You should have known you wouldn't get by with that trick."

Dolby liked sleeping on Bo's bed. Bo took him up-stairs, pointed to the rumpled covers, and said, "Stay, Dolby, stay." Leaping onto the bed, turning around three times, Dolby curled up and rested his chin on his paws. This wasn't punishment. He was ready for a nap.

About mid-morning, Dolby came and barked at Bo through the screen door. Bo ran to answer the phone, but he found it still on the hook. Dolby just wanted out. "Go back to sleep, Dolby. Go back upstairs. I know you want to go outside, but you're in trouble, remember?" Bo watched until Dolby started toward the bed-room.

The whole family worked hard. They stopped only for a snack, which Mrs. Dibbs brought out to the picnic table. Dolby was allowed out then, and Bo gave him a Woofies treat.

When they'd cleaned up for a late lunch and were ready to sit down to sandwiches that Ollie and Alice had prepared, Mr. Dibbs said, "It's funny that Dan Malcowitz hasn't called me. He said he'd call whether or not he had any news." He stared at the phone. "Maybe I should have turned on the answering machine, but I wanted to talk to him, and I'm sure one of us would have heard it ring. I'll try to reach him after we eat."

Ollie looked at Bo. Bo raised one eyebrow. It was a new trick he'd been practicing, raising only the eyebrow that wasn't under his patch. He was getting pretty good at it.

Mrs. Dibbs passed around a big bowl of salad and a bag of cookies. Everyone was extra hungry, and soon the phone call was forgotten.

Alice began telling about plans for junior high graduation. Bo was only half-listening, staring out the window and planning a Dolby training session after lunch. Suddenly, the doorbell rang.

"I'll get it!" Bo jumped up. Maybe it was Mr. Marzano with special news about the Woof-Off contest. He could see a man with a cap like the mail carrier's standing at the front door.

It wasn't Mr. Marzano. "Telegram for Mr. Dibbs." The man handed Bo a yellow envelope. "Sign here for your father." Handing Bo a pencil, the man pointed to a line with an X beside it. Bo printed his name quickly and dashed back to the kitchen table.

"It's a telegram!" he shouted. "A telegram. I never thought they'd send a telegram. But it's addressed to you, Dad. Open it!" Bo jumped up and down and clapped his hands. "Hurry and open it. Why didn't they address it to Dolby?"

"That's funny." Mr. Dibbs took the telegram. "No one sends a telegram these days. They call or send overnight letters or a FAX. Of course, we don't have a FAX machine here."

Bo hung over his father's shoulder as Mr. Dibbs ripped open the envelope. From his father's frown, however, Bo realized the telegram wasn't about Dolby being a finalist. He slid back down into his seat at the table and waited to find out what was written on the paper.

"Is it bad news, Howard?" Mrs. Dibbs stopped eating, her fork halfway to her mouth. "It's not about your father, is it?"

Mr. Dibbs finally spoke. "It's from Dan. He needed to get my advice this morning. He says he tried for hours to phone me but the line was busy. Finally, he made the decision himself, but he wanted me to know about it, and to know why he didn't call as we'd planned."

Ollie looked at Bo. Alice looked at Bo. Bo looked at the phone. No, it was definitely on the hook.

"Bo, would you go see if the bedroom extension is off the hook?" Mr. Dibbs demanded. The tone of voice he used said it had better not be.

"Yes, sir." Bo got up and climbed the stairs slowly. Dolby jumped up and followed him.

Sure enough, the phone in his parents' bedroom was lying on the floor.

"Woof-woof," said Dolby to Bo, sitting down and thumping his tail on the floor. *"Woof-woof."*

8

The Untraining of Dolby

After hanging up the phone, Bo walked slowly downstairs.

"Well, Bo," said his father, "was the phone off the hook up there?"

"Yes." Bo hung his head.

"All right. Who used the phone in our room? Who left the phone off?" Mr. Dibbs looked right at Alice.

"Don't look at me," Alice said quickly. "I have my own phone now, remember? Besides, I was outside with everyone else."

Ollie looked at Bo. "I think I know who did it, Dad," he said.

"Who?"

"Dolby."

Bo knew he should have been the one to tell that it was Dolby, but he was glad Ollie had done it for him. He couldn't escape being punished now, but maybe he wouldn't have to explain how this had happened. He'd probably be grounded forever, or at least all summer. Maybe his dad would even say he couldn't enter the Woof-Off. He sat down and slid lower into his chair.

"Dolby left the phone off the hook?" Mr. Dibbs was astonished. For a moment, he said nothing. "Well, I've seen you kids pass the blame before, but this beats all. You know Dolby didn't do any such thing."

"Yes, he did, Dad." Bo couldn't stay quiet any longer. "Dolby answers the phone all the time. It's a new trick I taught him. This morning, he came to get me. I checked the kitchen phone, but it wasn't off the hook, so I thought Dolby wanted to go back outside. This is all my fault."

"Start from the beginning, Bo," said Mrs. Dibbs, putting down her fork and pushing aside her plate.

"Well, you know how I'm teaching Dolby to do tricks for the Woof-Off. I taught him to answer the phone. I was hoping he'd even answer the call saying he was a finalist in the regional contest. He answers the phone, woofs, and then he comes and gets me."

"I don't believe it," said Mr. Dibbs.

Just then, the phone rang. Dolby started for it, and Bo grabbed his collar. Everyone seemed frozen in place as the phone rang again.

"Let him go," said Mr. Dibbs.

Bo let go of Dolby's collar, and on the third ring, the big dog put his paws on the counter, carefully lifted the receiver, placed it on the floor, and woofed. Then he turned and looked at the whole family, waiting for applause, or at least a Woofies Snack.

Mr. Dibbs put one hand to his head and took a deep breath. His lips pulled together into a tight line. Bo stopped watching and ran to answer the call.

"It's for you, Dad." He held out the receiver after wiping the dog spit on his T-shirt.

Slowly, Mr. Dibbs got up and answered the phone. "Yes, Dan," he said to the man on the other end of the line. "Yes, I got your message. Well, I'll explain it in a minute. Hold on; I'll go upstairs and talk to you. Would someone hang up here when I call out?"

Alice looked at Bo with an "I told you so" expression. Ollie's face was sympathetic. He'd had a lot of great ideas go wrong, too, so he knew how Bo felt. Mrs. Dibbs toyed with her food, her hand over her mouth. Dolby still sat in the middle of the kitchen floor, tongue lolling over his jaw, waiting for his Woofies Doggie Snack as reward for performing so well.

"Maybe you had better put Dolby outside for a few minutes, Bo," said Mrs. Dibbs. "And eat the rest of your lunch."

"I'm not very hungry." Bo got up and went outside with Dolby. The two of them sat on the back step. Bo put his arm around the big dog. "I'm going to get killed, Dolby . . . or grounded forever."

They listened to the buzz of flies and honeybees. The smell of a barbecue floated over from next door. Bo huddled closer to Dolby.

Finally, Mr. Dibbs came out and sat beside them. For a minute, all three sat in silence.

"Son, everything is all right at work, but it might not have been. This could have caused me a lot of problems."

"You might not have gotten rich," Bo guessed.

"Well, I'm not going to get rich anyway, but this was a very important business deal. As it turns out, the decision that Dan made was the one I would have advised, too. You have to understand, though, that phones aren't to play with."

"Dolby wasn't playing. He was a good answerer. He came and got me every time. We didn't miss any calls. It was just that this time, he answered the upstairs phone, and I didn't think about that."

"Sometimes it pays to think about things ahead of time, to think about how something that seems great might go wrong. What kind of punishment do you think this behavior deserves?"

"I guess I could be grounded forever." Bo hated to suggest that, but it seemed fair.

"Maybe not forever, but a week should give you time to think this over. And, Bo, as great a trick as this is, you have to help Dolby unlearn it."

"Teach Dolby *not* to answer the phone?" Bo would rather be grounded forever.

"That's right."

"It might be hard."

"No harder than it was to teach him the trick in the

first place. You can use the week you are grounded to do it."

From past experience, Bo knew it was harder to untrain Dolby than it was to train him. No matter how often Ollie or Bo told him not to, he always ran after Mrs. Mitchell's apricot poodle, Raggs, when he got a chance. And he liked to bark at Truffles if he wasn't loose to chase him. Dolby knew he wasn't supposed to chase cats or other dogs, but he liked doing it. Now he liked answering the phone. It would be hard to break him of the habit.

"I'll try, Dad," Bo promised. He was glad he and Dolby hadn't ruined his father's business deal.

"Try very hard." Mr. Dibbs got up and went inside.

That night, when Bo and Ollie went to bed, Ollie said, "I'm sorry your great idea went wrong, Bo. At least you know that Dolby was able to learn it. It can go down in Dolby's repertoire of best tricks ever."

"Yeah, I guess so."

On Monday after school, Bo got to work untraining Dolby. Although Bo had to stay in his yard and have no company, he figured he could still talk to his friends on the phone. He hadn't told anyone except Alvin and Gary about the trouble he and Dolby were in. It was too embarrassing. He needed Alvin's help desperately, though. Over and over, he had Alvin call. When Dolby started to answer the phone, Bo would shout, "No, Dolby, no. That game is over. Don't answer the phone. No, Dolby, no."

At first, Dolby just looked at Bo with a question in his eyes. Then he'd start to do the trick, anyway. Bo had to find the water pistol they'd used to train Dolby when he was a puppy. Dolby hated water in his face, so that worked pretty well. Bo felt awful, though. He knew Dolby didn't understand why he had to unlearn this trick.

As much as possible, he kept Dolby in the yard with the back door closed. They worked on other tricks all week. They worked especially hard on *fetch*. Dolby could fetch a ball, a stick, and finally the handkerchief on command. Bo hugged him especially hard the first time he got the handkerchief.

Over and over, Bo practiced crying. While his face was in his hands, he'd whisper, "Fetch the handkerchief, Dolby, the handkerchief." Again and again, Dolby picked up the bandanna and handed it to Bo.

Dolby would probably never understand why he had to stop doing the neat phone trick, but since Bo kept scolding him and stopped rewarding him, he began to get the idea.

Once when Dolby forgot and answered the telephone, Bo sat him on the back step and gave him a lecture. "Dolby, I know you don't understand why you have to unlearn this trick, but it's important. If you don't, Dad might say you can't be in the Woof-Off. You don't want that to happen, do you?"

Dolby's ears perked up. He turned his head sideways.

"I'd cry if you didn't get to be in the Woof-Off," said Bo, and he pretended to cry, trying a new twist to the handkerchief trick. He'd put the bandanna in plain sight in his pocket.

Dolby put his paw in Bo's lap and whined. Through his fingers, Bo said, "Fetch, Dolby, fetch the handkerchief." Not fooled by where it was placed, Dolby pulled the bandanna from Bo's pocket and handed it to him.

"Good dog, Dolby. Good dog!" Bo tossed Dolby a Woofies Snack. He'd keep thinking of some more tricks for Dolby. There was time before the contest. He still didn't know whether or not Dolby was a finalist, but it was good he hadn't waited to find out. With only three weeks left, he would never have had time to plan a good routine. Besides, the more new tricks he taught Dolby, the more likely he'd be to forget the phone trick.

On Saturday morning, after his week of being grounded was over, Bo was trying to decide what to do. He hadn't heard from the contest people, but he wasn't going to give up.

Ollie knew that his brother had worked hard on both Dolby's training and untraining. "I'm going over to C-Mart, Bo. Want to come with me?"

Bo jumped up. "Yes. Can Dolby go?"

"Sure. He probably needs a walk."

"Yeah, fetching isn't that much exercise when you have to stay in the yard." Bo got Dolby's leash. Pretty soon, they were headed down the bike trail, Dolby in the lead.

"It's really hard to untrain a dog, isn't it, Ollie?" asked

74

Bo. Last night, just when Bo had thought he'd successfully broken Dolby of answering the phone, he'd gotten away twice and picked up the receiver. The second time was right in front of Mr. Dibbs.

"Yeah, but Dolby's smart. He'll catch on before long. You just have to keep him from doing it for another week or so."

"Okay. I'm trying, Ollie."

Bo had a good hold on Dolby's leash, but the big dog tugged so hard, Bo was practically running. Dolby loved being out of his yard. There were so many new things to see and such great smells. He trotted along, his nose to the ground, the bushes, and the new flowers neighbors had planted. He barked at people running on the bicycle trail, and at Frank's collie, Basher, who lived behind the field and at the corner where the bike trail joined the street again. He barked at Sheri Long-holtz, who waved at them. She was still twirling her baton. She tossed it in the air, but she still couldn't catch it.

Ollie took Bo's hand when they had to cross the busy intersection at Twenty-eighth Street.

"Can Dolby and I stay out here and watch the prairie dogs?" asked Bo when they got to C-Mart. "Dogs aren't allowed in the store, anyway."

Bo was proud of the prairie-dog village. He felt that it was really Ollie's. Ollie had helped to save the prairie dogs when people wanted to get rid of them. He'd protested plans to kill or move them, and he'd talked the developers into making this a protected place for them to play. Also, it was a way for people to see the prairie dogs and learn about their habits.

Ollie looked around. There were several children standing with their parents, watching the prairie dogs. "I guess so. But be sure not to speak to any strangers, Bo."

"I promise, Ollie. And I'll stand right there until you come back out."

Bo thought prairie dogs were just about the funniest animals in the world to watch. He tried to count how many were in the village, which had all sorts of tiny houses, bridges, and miniature playground equipment where the animals could play.

Dolby started to bark at the prairie dogs as they stood beside their holes watching the people watch them.

"Hush, Dolby, hush," Bo scolded. "Sit down. You'll scare them." He kept a tight hold on Dolby's leash even though there was a fence around the village.

The prairie dogs yipped and fell over backward. Bo laughed. This was his favorite of all their habits. Dolby lay down after a few minutes, and Bo relaxed his hold on the leash. There were some babies already. Bo tried to make a count of them. The babies imitated their parents. Bo leaned over as two of them got closer and closer to the fence. He knew the mothers would chase after them.

"Seven, eight—" Bo counted.

Suddenly, a noise sounded in the distance. At first, Bo paid no attention to it, but Dolby did. He sat up.

His ears stood up, and he looked around. Then he started to quiver. It was a sound he was supposed to ignore, part of a trick he was supposed to stop doing. The temptation was too great, though.

Dolby jumped up and took off across the parking lot.

"Dolby, come back!" Bo yelled. He started after the big dog, then tripped and fell.

By the time Bo got up, brushed off his skinned hands, swallowed the lump in his throat, and blinked back the tears in his eyes, he saw where Dolby was headed.

There was a row of pay phones outside of C-Mart, and one of them was ringing.

9
Big News

Before Bo could reach Dolby, the big dog had answered the phone. The receiver was dangling on its cord. Dolby woofed into the mouthpiece. *Woof-woof. Wait a minute.* Two boys stepped out of the second phone booth. One was Lester Philpott.

Bo raced up, panting.

"Good dog, Dolby," said Lester, giving Dolby half his peanut-butter cup. "Good dog. Boy, it's great the way he learned that trick, isn't it, Bo? I saw you guys and wondered if I would get Dolby to answer the phone over here. I wanted Clarence to see it. He wouldn't believe me." A tall, skinny boy stood beside Lester, grinning. "Think of Dolby answering the pay phone outside C-Mart, Clarence. I'm going to tell everyone at school about it."

"He's supposed to be unlearning it, Lester," Bo said in a trembling voice. "You knew that."

"Unlearning it? I didn't, Bo, honest I didn't. I thought I was helping you out." Lester licked the chocolate off his fingers. Dolby watched hopefully. "What happened? How come Dolby has to unlearn such a great trick?"

"It's a long story," said Bo quietly, sitting on the curb. He held back his tears until Lester and Clarence swung onto their bicycles and pedaled away. "Maybe Lester really didn't know," Bo said to Dolby.

Now Dolby was trained again. There was nothing like a peanut-butter cup to undo Bo's hard work. Tears streamed down Bo's face, and he didn't try to hold them back. Dolby whined while Bo really cried.

"What's the matter, Bo?" Ollie called, running from the store with his package.

"Lester called Dolby on that phone and said 'Good dog' when he answered. He gave him candy and now Dolby's trained again," Bo said through his tears.

"I'm sorry, Bo," said Ollie, sitting down on the curb beside Bo. "It sounds as if Lester thought he was helping you. He couldn't have known you got in trouble over the trick unless you told everyone at school. It's too late to do anything. You'll just have to work harder with Dolby. But be careful what you teach him next. Think before you act."

"I'll try, Ollie," Bo said. He hadn't told everyone. Even when he told Alvin and Gary, he made them promise not to tell anyone else. He wrapped Dolby's leash around his sore hand and they started for home.

Ollie checked the mailbox at the curb when they

reached the Dibbses' driveway. "There's a letter for you, Bo," he said. "It's from the Woof-Off people."

"The Woof-Off people! It's good news. I know it is." Bo grabbed the letter, then knew he was too nervous to sound out all the words he didn't know. "You read it, Ollie." Bo handed back the envelope when they got in the kitchen.

Ollie opened the letter. "Dear Bo Dibbs and Dolby," he started. "We are most impressed with the recording you sent us of Dolby's voice. We are pleased to inform you that Dolby is one of the finalists for the regional Woof-Off to be held at Sacred Heart School in Boulder, Colorado, on Saturday, May twenty-fifth. We assume you read the rules on the Woofies Dog Food bag, but enclosed is a duplicate copy. Please let us know if you cannot participate in the finals."

"Wow!" Bo threw the letter in the air. It made up for all the problems he was having. Nothing was going to keep Dolby from attending the finals in Cincinnati. Bo was sure Dolby would win.

"Woof-Off, Woof-Off, Woof-Off. Dolby's in the Woof-Off." Bo sang and danced around the kitchen. Dolby knew something exciting had happened. He barked and danced with Bo.

Finally, Bo stopped and gave Dolby a hug. "They're impressed with your woof. What did I tell you? Speak, Dolby, speak," Bo said.

"*Woof-woof, woof-woof.*" Dolby was glad to bark.

"Pretend you're a Woof-Off judge, Ollie," Bo begged. "Just for a few minutes, please."

"All right. Just for a few minutes, Bo," Ollie agreed.

Ollie stood straight, looking over the audience watching the Woof-Off. "And now for our final contestant, Dolby Dibbs."

"Say Dolby, the Wonder Dog," prompted Bo.

"The judge won't say that," Ollie reminded Bo. "We'd better do this just like the real thing."

"Okay." Bo was disappointed, but he knew Ollie was right. "Now, I'll lead Dolby up to the judge. Come on, Dolby."

Bo snapped on Dolby's leash. The dog sat looking back and forth at Ollie and Bo.

"Stand up, Dolby. You have to stand straight and walk calmly up to the judge."

Dolby stood up for Bo, even though he was ready for another nap. The walk from C-Mart and all the excitement in the kitchen had made him tired.

"Fine dog you have there, Mr. Dibbs," said Ollie the judge.

"Thank you. He can do lots of tricks, too." Bo put his hand beside his mouth. "I'm going to save woofing for last," he whispered to Ollie. "Roll over, Dolby. Now play dead." Bo put Dolby through some of his tricks. Dolby didn't want to stop playing dead, since that was also his sleeping position, but Bo made him get up. "Now speak, Dolby, speak." Dolby barked again, but not with much enthusiasm. "He'll do better at the contest," Bo told Ollie. "I think he's getting tired."

Ollie nodded. "And the winner is . . ." Ollie paused for dramatic effect. "The winner is Dolby, the Wonder

Dog. Congratulations, Mr. Dibbs. This is a fine dog you have here. He'll have to star in many commercials, you know. I assume he already eats Woofies?"

"Oh, yes." Bo had unloaded his pocket, rewarding Dolby for the practice contest. "He eats lots of Woofies and recommends Woofies Dog Food to all his friends."

Ollie and Bo laughed, and Dolby went to sleep immediately after the show.

On Saturday afternoon, Bo decided he could do more with Dolby's ability to fetch. After all, he was half retriever and that was what retrievers did best. He knew the word really well now. Bo decided to build his whole show around the command *fetch*.

It was a big snake year in the neighborhood. Twice more while Dolby was fetching a ball, he brought back a snake instead. Bo ran upstairs and dug in his toy box. Once he had had a plastic snake. He found it. He also grabbed Paddington Bear. He had learned to sleep without it, but he decided he'd never part with his bear. It had been too good a friend.

Out in the yard, he reminded Dolby what each thing was. "Snake," he said over and over, showing Dolby the plastic snake. Then he repeated *bear* until Dolby knew the difference. He set them side by side. "Fetch the snake, Dolby."

Dolby grabbed the snake and took it to Bo, green ends wiggling out of each side of his mouth. Bo took it from him and put it back.

"Bear, Dolby, fetch the bear." Bo hoped Paddington wouldn't mind a little dog spit on his coat.

Dolby had a little trouble picking up the big bear, but he made the right choice.

"Now the ball, Dolby, the ball."

Quickly, Dolby ran after the ball. He'd known that word for a long time.

"Good dog, Dolby, good dog." One, two, three Woofies sailed into the air. *Snap, snap, snap.* Dolby loved Woofies. The judges wouldn't doubt that.

"Take a nap, Dolby, sleep. A nap. Lie down. I need something to drink. Be right back."

Dolby obeyed gratefully, lying in the shade while Bo took a break.

"How's the training coming?" asked Mrs. Dibbs, pouring Bo some lemonade.

"Great, just great, Mom. We're very close to being ready." After Bo had finished his drink, he returned to the yard and found trouble. Dolby was no longer napping. In fact, he was gone.

Before Bo could look around, he heard screaming.

"Stop, Dolby, stop!" Sheri Longholtz yelled as she chased Dolby across the field behind Bo's house. Her friend Irene Keeble tried to head Dolby off, but he was good at dodging.

Dolby skidded to a stop at Bo's feet. There was something in his mouth. A tail dangled from one corner. Bo reached in, thinking he'd find a snake. Why would Sheri and Irene be chasing Dolby to get a snake?

It wasn't a snake. Inside Dolby's mouth, Bo found a very damp baby kitten. It was so small, it didn't even have its eyes open.

"Dolby ate my kitten." Sheri continued to scream. Then she burst into sobs.

"Sheri, he didn't," Bo said, holding out the marmalade-colored baby. "It's fine, really. He just fetched it. I didn't tell him to, honest I didn't. It was Dolby's idea." Bo didn't say "Good dog" to Dolby, since he didn't want this to happen again. He didn't scold him, though, because he didn't want Dolby to unlearn *fetch*.

"You did, too, Bo Dibbs. You sent Dolby over to my house just for meanness. Boys are always doing mean things. You knew I had baby kittens. I told about it at show-and-tell on Friday. Now Dolby has killed one."

"He didn't, really, Sheri," said Irene, taking the baby from Bo. "Look at it." The kitten opened its tiny mouth and mewed. Its head bobbed up and down.

Sheri calmed down when she saw the kitten was okay.

"I think it was partly Fiona's fault," said Irene. "She keeps moving her babies."

"I can't believe Dolby went clear into your yard, Sheri. I just left him asleep in my yard. And he never runs away."

"I—I—he didn't, Bo." Sheri wiped the tears off her cheeks. "I just said that because I was upset. Maybe since it isn't hurt, I should thank Dolby. I couldn't find this one. We were searching the field when I saw Dolby pick up something. Then I heard it cry. Good dog, Dolby." Sheri patted Dolby. "Good dog. You rescued the baby for me. Fiona was bad to take it in the field."

Bo smiled. He felt very relieved. Even though Dolby was finding things to fetch on his own, Bo had no more time for untraining him. "Dolby really doesn't like cats, but maybe he knew this one was lost, since it was so little. I hope Fiona doesn't mind a little dog spit on her baby."

"So do I," said Sheri. "Thanks, Bo. Thanks, Dolby. You're a really smart dog. I'm sure you'll win the Woof-Off." She and Irene waved to Bo and Dolby as they ran home.

10

Contest Day

"Look," Bo said a week later. "Dolby's name is in the Sunday newspaper. Con-tes-tants." Bo sounded out the word. "Dolby Dibbs. See, right here." Bo carried the newspaper article around to everyone in his family. Later that day, he showed Alvin and Gary.

Ollie's friends were looking forward to the event, too. Frank Ashburn had groomed his collie so often, Ollie teased him that Basher was going to be bald by the day of the contest.

When Bo went to his eye doctor on Monday, he found out that even Dr. Norbert was excited.

"Truffles is a finalist, too, Bo. May the best dog win." Dr. Norbert put out his hand to Bo. Bo shook it and wished him luck. Although, since he knew Dolby was going to win, he felt as if he wasn't being truthful.

Bo was able to take his patch off just in time. He'd gotten used to it, but he wasn't looking forward to wearing it in front of a big crowd. He was going to have to wear glasses, but that made him feel even luckier about the contest. He was getting more like Ollie every day. He had overcome all the disasters, or near-disasters, he'd come across in the training of Dolby. Ollie often had things go wrong, but he never gave up when he was trying to accomplish something. Bo had never given up, even when his best trick had gone wrong.

And Ollie nearly always won. Bo was going to win the Woof-Off with Dolby. He'd be just as famous as Ollie. People would say to Mr. and Mrs. Dibbs, "How does it feel to have two famous sons?" Alice might not like it if she overheard the question, but Bo didn't think Alice cared whether she was famous or not. Maybe having famous brothers was enough.

At dinner, three days before the Woof-Off, Mr. Dibbs reminded them that he would be gone over the weekend.

"Bo, your mom and I sure hate to miss the event of the season. You do remember that our team has to be in Mexico this weekend, don't you? And your mother has to supervise the tests of her new computers all weekend."

"I remember, Dad. But we can still go with Alice, can't we?" Bo's stomach gave a wiggle. Please, please, don't let anything else go wrong.

"Mom, I know I said I'd go with Bo and Ollie on Saturday, but that was a long time ago, before I started going out with Hamilton. We want to help decorate for the fifties sock hop the school is having on Saturday night."

"I realize that, Alice. And I'm glad you have a friend you like, but you know how much Bo has counted on this contest."

"Don't you want to see Dolby win the Woof-Off, Alice?" Bo asked.

Alice looked at Bo. His long face was getting longer. One tear ran down his cheek. "Oh, good grief!" She looked as if she was going to cry herself. "Hamilton Byers has finally invited me to something really special. Ollie's old enough to look after Bo in the daytime." Alice tried one more time.

"Yeah, Mom, I'm going. We'll be all right. I'll look after Bo and Dolby." Ollie knew he watched after Bo a lot, anyway.

"I don't feel right about Ollie and Bo going over there alone," said Mr. Dibbs. "If this boy is the kind of boy we'd want you going out with, Alice, he won't mind going to the Woof-Off with you. Sacred Heart is right next to Casey Junior High. You can still go over there after the contest and get in some decorating."

"Take two little brothers and a dog to the gym with me? Ask Hamilton to go to the Woof-Off? Gross! I'm going back to bed and stay there for a week."

"Sure. Let's take Hamilton to the Woof-Off." Bo brightened up. "He'd love seeing Dolby win. Then we'll all help decorate."

"*Woof-woof.*" Dolby looked right at Alice as if he knew what all the fuss was about.

"Good grief!" Alice jumped up from the table and went into the kitchen to stare out the window.

"Call Hamilton, dear," said Mrs. Dibbs. "If he says no, we'll try to think of something else. Maybe Mrs. Rumwinkle is free. She'd probably enjoy the contest."

"She's allergic to dogs, remember?" said Ollie. "Even though Dolby stays in the garage, she sneezes a lot. She'd have to be around dozens of dogs at the contest."

Alice ran upstairs, leaving her dinner.

"I don't think Alice wants to go," said Bo, pushing his green beans around on his plate.

"Frank's mother is going," said Ollie. "We could go with them."

"I can't ask Mrs. Ashburn to watch after three boys and two dogs," said Mrs. Dibbs.

After a few minutes, Alice returned. She sat at the dining table and toyed with her food.

"What did he say?" Bo finally asked.

Alice took a deep breath. "He said—he said he thought it would be fun."

"Yea!" Bo jumped up and down.

"Well, that's settled." Mrs. Dibbs sighed. "Eat your dinner, Bo."

"I'll be eager to find out how Dolby does in the competition," said Mr. Dibbs. "I'll call you if I can. I've told everyone at work. They said to wish you luck."

Bo knew his dad and mom wanted to go. It wasn't

the first time they'd had to miss something because of their jobs. The family had talked several times about problems that came up because both Mr. and Mrs. Dibbs worked. Mrs. Dibbs liked her job as much as Mr. Dibbs liked his. Sometimes she said computers were easier to work with than people.

"Yeah, Dad, it's okay. I know you can't postpone a solar eclipse. I'm sorry you can't go." Bo slipped Dolby a piece of pot roast.

"Will you have Dolby perform for us, Bo?" asked Mr. Dibbs. "For the whole family?"

"Right now?" asked Bo.

"Sure, I want to see the act, too." Mrs. Dibbs turned her chair around. "Pretend the kitchen is the stage."

"I'll be the announcer." Ollie jumped up. "I did it once before."

"Yeah, but the act is better, Ollie." Bo stood up. "Wait and see." He ran upstairs to get the props for his act. When he returned, he motioned to Ollie that he was ready.

"Announcing Bo Dibbs and Dolby," Ollie began. He made the same speech he'd practiced before.

Bo snapped on Dolby's leash. He led him to the kitchen, which was in full view of the audience of four.

First, he had Dolby sit, roll over, play dead—his ordinary tricks. Dolby performed beautifully, always catching his Woofie treat.

Then Bo had Dolby sit and stay while he placed around the room a tennis ball, the plastic snake, and a worn-out fuzzy kitten toy he'd found in one of Ollie's garage-sale boxes. He'd thought of adding the kitten after Dolby rescued Fiona's baby.

Walking back to Dolby, Bo said, "Fetch the ball, Dolby, the ball."

Dolby cocked his head, looked at Bo, then trotted off toward the ball. He brought it back, handed it to Bo, and swallowed his treat.

"Now fetch the snake, Dolby, the snake."

Dolby looked around. Bo held his breath. Then Dolby trotted over, picked up the green plastic snake, and took it to Bo.

"Good dog, Dolby, good dog!" Bo tossed Dolby a Woofie treat as he praised him. "Now fetch the kitten, Dolby, the kitten." Bo said the word *kitten* very clearly. He'd made sure never to call it a cat. He wondered if Dolby knew a kitten was a cat.

Dolby raced for the remaining toy.

"All right, Dolby . . ." Bo paused for dramatic effect. "Fetch the bear, the bear."

"But Bo . . ." Ollie whispered.

"It's all right, Ollie," Bo whispered back. "Watch. The bear, Dolby, the bear."

Dolby looked all around the edge of the kitchen. He even looked in the audience, licking up a crumb from under the table, but he returned to Bo with nothing in his mouth.

By that time, Bo had folded his legs Indian-style and was sitting down. He had the bandanna in his shirt pocket. "Oh, you failed, Dolby, you failed." Bo started to cry.

Dolby pawed at Bo, whined, then pulled out the handkerchief and gave it to Bo. Bo blew his nose loudly while slipping Dolby a treat. Then he bowed.

The audience went wild. They clapped and stomped their feet and Alice whistled. When it got quiet, Ollie said, "Good show, Mr. Dibbs. But does Dolby have a good bark?"

"Speak, Dolby, speak," commanded Bo.

"Woof-woof, woof-woof." Dolby barked beautifully to another round of applause.

"And the winner is"—Ollie paused—"Dolby, the Wonder Dog, trained by Bo Dibbs, the world's best dog trainer."

Bo, Ollie, and Dolby bowed.

"Good show!" said Mr. Dibbs, clapping again. "This is almost as good as an eclipse."

"Yeah," Ollie added. "Dolby will eclipse the competition."

"Oh, Bo," said Mrs. Dibbs. "How can such a great act lose?"

Saturday arrived at last. Bo hoped Dolby was ready. He had given him a bath after school on Friday. Dolby hated baths, so it was always a big job.. After one more session with the grooming brush, Bo pronounced Dolby ready.

"Dolby looks great, Bo," said Hamilton Byers. He had walked to the Dibbses' house to accompany them to Sacred Heart School. Alice had taken forever to get ready to go, but now she stood on the other side of

Hamilton, pretending she didn't know any of the rest of them.

Gary and Alvin ran into the backyard. "We're ready," they said together.

"You're going with us, too?" asked Alice.

"We can't miss this, Alice," said Alvin.

"It's the greatest thing that's happened to anyone I know," said Gary.

"Good grief," said Alice, closing her eyes and taking a deep breath.

"Dolby's going to win the Woof-Off, Hamilton," said Bo when they started off, looking like a parade. "Just wait and see. You'll be proud of him."

Ollie had given Bo all the advice he could think of. "We're all going to be proud," he said, "no matter what happens. Think how many dogs didn't make it to the regional contest."

Rebecca met them at the corner of her street. "I wouldn't miss the Woof-Off for anything," Rebecca said. "Good luck, Bo."

"I don't need luck, Rebecca, but thanks," Bo replied. "We've practiced. Not only does Dolby have the best woof but he's going to be the best-behaved dog and know the best tricks." Bo patted Dolby on the head to remind him of that.

"I guess a lot of other dog owners plan to win, too," Hamilton reminded Bo.

"Yeah, but we aren't worried." Bo held Dolby's leash tightly as he was tugged along.

To Bo's surprise, Lester and Clarence were at the

gym. "Hi, Bo," said Lester. "I'm sure Dolby will win today. I hurried to finish my paper route so I could watch."

"Thanks, Lester," Bo said.

"What is Lester doing here?" asked Alice.

"I guess he just wanted to watch Dolby perform," said Ollie.

"He's being nice, isn't he, Ollie?" asked Bo. "He wants Dolby to win, too."

There was a huge crowd at the gym. Many people had cameras. The local television station had brought its Minicams. The mayor and some of the city council were there. At one end of the gym, the Woofies Dog Food people had set up a small stage with both a high microphone and one that was low.

"The little microphone is for the dogs," Bo guessed.

"What if he won't woof when they tell him to?" asked Rebecca. "What will you do, Bo?"

"That would never happen, Rebecca," Bo assured her. "Dolby is excited, and he always barks when he's excited." Dolby barked to prove what Bo had said. "Shhh, Dolby, not yet." Bo hushed Dolby.

Bo saw Dr. Norbert sitting with his wife and baby. He was holding Truffles in his lap. Bo wondered if the judges would like a yip-yip like Truffles had or a deep, bass-drum woof-woof like Dolby's bark. Neither Bo nor Dolby much liked yip-yip dogs. Surely Dolby wouldn't try to chase Truffles during the contest. Even so, Bo hoped Truffles wouldn't be standing anywhere near Dolby when it was their turn.

There were a lot of things that Bo could worry about, but he had promised himself he wouldn't worry. He had confidence in Dolby. Worrying would make him nervous, and if he was nervous, Dolby would know it. That would make Dolby nervous.

"Good dog, Dolby, good dog." Bo made Dolby sit on the floor in front of the first row of bleachers, where all the contestants had a special place to sit. Friends had to sit up behind them, except that Ollie squeezed in next to Bo in case he needed help with Dolby. If Dolby took a notion to misbehave, it would be hard for Bo to stop him.

Bo wished they could be first. His number was nineteen. He counted. All twenty-five dogs were there. That meant they were nearly last. It would take a long time to get to him and Dolby.

"Lie down, Dolby," Bo said. "Lie down. I think he'll do better if he takes a nap now," Bo whispered to Ollie.

The first two dogs were ordinary. "No competition there," whispered Ollie.

"Nope," said Bo.

Truffles was third. He jumped through a hoop, turned three back flips in a row, rolled over, sat up, played dead, then yipped into the microphone. His shrill voice made Bo cover his ears. "Not bad if you like yip-yip dogs," he whispered to Ollie.

"They won't," said Ollie. "They'll want a big, sophisticated dog."

Bo looked at Dolby. His tongue had lolled out of his mouth in his sleep and his legs were twitching. He was chasing rabbits or cats or yip-yip dogs in his dream. He didn't look much like a TV star. Bo poked him, and Dolby scrambled to his feet.

"No, it's not your turn, Dolby," Bo said in his ear. "But pay attention now. You can see what you have to do."

They all paid attention as a big, fancy dog walked to the front to take his turn. The dog was a purebred Great Dane, not a mixed breed like Dolby. His brown coat was sleek, polished-looking. He stood tall, holding his head and his stub of a tail high.

His name was Duke. First, he did tricks that almost all the dogs knew, like rolling over and playing dead. Then he jumped through three hoops placed at a distance. Next, he jumped three hurdles, also spaced several steps apart. Duke sailed over each jump perfectly, turned, and sailed back, bouncing once and scrunching for the next jump between each. Dolby barked at the end of that trick as if to say, Good show.

"Hush, Dolby," said Bo. "Just watch."

"Yeah, no comments," said Hamilton, who sat behind Bo, laughing.

Duke paid no attention to his audience but kept his owners, a young husband-and-wife team, busy helping him show off. He counted toy monkeys by tapping his foot, then gave the three monkeys a ride on a little saddle fastened to his back. Over the hurdles and through the hoops, Duke jumped.

"Show-off," whispered Lester from his seat two rows above them.

Bo nodded his agreement. "It must have taken years to teach him to do all that. The judges will probably decide he's too old."

When Duke woofed perfectly, a deep, impressive woof, Bo started to worry. Sweat dripped down his cheeks, and he wiggled on his hard seat.

Long before Dolby's turn, the gym became hot and smelled very doggy. Pretty soon, Bo started yawning. Every finalist seemed to take a long time. After Duke, none of the dogs was as good as he had been. Bo had to keep his faith, though. Dolby's tricks were better than jumping. Most dogs could jump over things, but how many could fetch on command? Jumping didn't require a big vocabulary like Dolby had now.

"Bo, I'm sorry," said Rebecca, climbing down and stopping in front of Dolby. She and Alvin and Gary had been sitting up high so they could see well. "I have to leave. I thought for sure Dolby would be finished by now. My mom is picking me up outside at eleven-thirty."

Gary's parents were picking him up, too, and he had to leave. "Good luck, Bo and Dolby. I'm still betting on you."

The crowd got smaller as each dog performed and some of his fan club left.

"I'm getting tired, Ollie," said Bo, yawning. "We've sure seen some good tricks, haven't we? And some good barking."

"Yeah," Ollie admitted. "But don't get discouraged, Bo. Dolby is just as good."

Bo had taken Dolby outside to the bathroom once. He and Ollie had left Dolby with Alice and found the boys' bathroom in the school twice. "It's because I'm nervous," Bo explained to Alice the second time.

"Good grief," said Alice, looking anywhere but at Hamilton Byers. "I wish they'd hurry up," she added.

Number eighteen was performing when Bo told Dolby to stand up. He looked Dolby over and smoothed his fur. "You'll do fine, Dolby," he said. "Now don't be nervous."

Bo's hand was shaking on Dolby's leash. His stomach felt as if fleas had left all the dogs and set up a circus in there. They were doing back flips when Dolby's number was called.

"Number nineteen," said the head judge. "Dolby Dibbs. Please come to the stage."

Immediately, Bo was full of energy. Any thought of being sleepy disappeared. Dolby felt the same way. He'd heard his name called, and Bo had said, "Come on, Dolby." Dolby pulled Bo toward the stage. Bo had insisted that Ollie let him take Dolby up alone to perform. Now Dolby was taking Bo toward the judges.

Suddenly, Dolby stopped. His ears perked up like twin mountain peaks. He started to shiver. He looked around. Bo tugged his leash to get him to pay attention.

The big dog hunched down and leaped. Jerking loose from Bo easily and leaving him behind, he spun around and took off down the middle of the gym floor. Then Dolby dashed eagerly for the gymnasium door.

11

The Phone Call

"Dolby, come back!" Bo yelled. "Come back!"

He dashed after the big dog, trying to step on his leash, but Dolby outdistanced Bo in seconds.

"What's the matter, Dolby?" yelled Ollie. He jumped up, but he was too late, too. He ran after Bo and Dolby.

From far down the hall, in the direction where Bo and Ollie had disappeared twice, Dolby had heard a noise he liked. He heard a noise he'd been taught to respond to. A phone was ringing.

Dolby had tried to ignore the ringing. He knew he wasn't supposed to answer the phone anymore, but the *brrrring-brrring-brrrring* kept on. Finally, he couldn't stand it anymore.

Down the long hall of the school raced Dolby, Bo, and Ollie.

The office door was open only a crack when Dolby reached it. No problem—he nosed it open and sped into the small room. On the secretary's desk, the phone jingled insistently.

Dolby put his paws up onto the desk, lifted the receiver of the phone carefully, and placed it on the desk. *"Woof-woof,"* he barked. *"Woof-woof."* Bo was right behind him. *"Woof-woof, Bo. Woof-woof."* Dolby looked at Bo and wagged his tail. His tongue lolled out the side of his mouth. He was proud of himself.

"Dolby!" Bo shouted. "Bad dog, bad dog." While Dolby ducked his head and his tail and sat down, Bo automatically picked up the phone. "Hello?"

There was a low humming noise at the end of the line.

"See that, Dolby." Bo was in tears. "They hung up. It was probably a wrong number, anyway."

Ollie stood watching everything. Bo started to cry harder. Ollie put his arms around Bo and hugged him close.

"He could have won, Ollie." Bo sobbed. "I know he could have won. You could have won, Dolby," Bo scolded the big dog. "You could have been famous. You could have been a big television star. You blew it, Dolby." Bo wiped his face and tried to stop crying.

"You missed the opportunity of a lifetime, Dolby," Ollie scolded. "You could have made a lot of money."

"I didn't care about the money, Ollie. I just wanted Dolby to be famous." Bo wanted to be famous, too, like Ollie. Now he'd never get another chance, and all because Dolby forgot and answered the phone. "I didn't even hear the phone, Ollie," Bo said. "Did you?"

"Dogs can hear that kind of sound better than we can, Bo. But all the way down here, Dolby? You win for dog with best hearing, I guess. It's too bad, Bo, but it's not your fault. It's Dolby's fault. He's just a dumb dog."

"No, he's smart, Ollie." Bo hugged Dolby. "He just forgot. But why now, Dolby?" Bo asked. "Why now?"

"I guess we can go home, Bo." Ollie took Bo's hand. "I'm sure Dolby was disqualified when he ran from the room."

"Yeah, I'm too embarrassed to go back in there, even if they'd let Dolby have another chance."

Before the boys could leave the office, the phone rang again. Dolby looked at Bo, but he didn't dare answer it. Bo looked at Ollie. Ollie shrugged. "We might as well answer. Hello," he said, picking up the phone.

"Yes, yes this is. We're in the office. Yes, he's here."

Bo listened to the one-sided conversation and wondered to whom Ollie was talking. Who would call Ollie here?

"Yes, I'll find him and give him the message." Ollie finished the conversation. "That was for Dr. Norbert. Come on; we've got to find him." Ollie took off down the hall. "He's supposed to go to the hospital. He's needed for an emergency."

Bo and Dolby followed Ollie back to the gym. Alice, Hamilton, and Alvin were waiting just outside the door.

"What happened, Bo?" Alvin asked. "Dolby blew it."

"I know it, Alvin. He went to answer the phone.

Would you hold Dolby, Alice?" Bo handed Alice Dolby's leash and followed Ollie.

They found Dr. Norbert easily. The eye doctor was still sitting near the front of the gym, although his wife and daughter were gone. Truffles, finished with his part in the competition, was napping near Dr. Norbert's feet. They were waiting to see who had won the contest.

"Dr. Norbert," Ollie said, "there's an emergency for you at the hospital. They said they'd tried to reach you."

Dr. Norbert automatically checked his beeper. He took it off his belt and switched it off and on. "Oh, no, I forgot to change the batteries this morning. It's probably dead."

"Where's Mrs. Norbert and your baby?" asked Bo.

"They just left. Ellen needed her nap, and they were tired. Listen, boys. Can you get Truffles home? I'd better go straight to the hospital."

"Sure," said Ollie, taking Truffles's leash.

"You won't know if he won," said Bo, remembering that the winner hadn't been announced. In fact, the contest was continuing while they talked.

"Can't be helped. I think Truffles is out of his league here. That Great Dane will probably win." Dr. Norbert pointed to Duke, who sat like a king watching everyone.

"Dolby won't win, that's for sure." Bo looked around, but everything became a blur.

"How did you boys happen to answer the phone?" asked Dr. Norbert as they headed out of the gym.

"It's a long story," said Ollie.

Dr. Norbert dashed for his car, leaving Truffles in

Ollie's care. Bo took Dolby and tightened his leash so the big dog wouldn't bother Truffles.

Neither boy felt like decorating for a party, so Alice and Hamilton made sure Ollie knew the way home.

"Don't accept any rides or speak to any strangers, Ollie," Alice reminded him.

"I won't, Alice. I'm smarter than that."

Alice didn't need to worry about Bo. He didn't feel like speaking to anyone.

"I'm sorry, Bo," said Hamilton, patting him on the shoulder. "What happened? Where did Dolby go so fast?"

"It's a long story." Bo repeated what Ollie had said to Dr. Norbert. "I'll tell you later."

"It's a tragedy," said Ollie after Alice and Hamilton had left them and they were on their way home.

"Yeah, a tragedy," Bo agreed.

"Yeah," echoed Alvin.

About a block from the Dibbses', Lester whizzed by on his bike. He popped a wheelie at the corner, spun around, and headed back for the boys and the dogs. Dolby barked as Lester skidded right in front of them. Truffles yip-yipped.

"Why did Dolby do that, Bo? Why did he leave the room just when it was his turn? I was sure he would win." Lester patted Dolby on the head.

"He got an important phone call." Alvin answered for Bo.

"I'm sorry he didn't win, Bo," Lester said, giving Alvin a funny look. "I'm sure he could have. Dolby's the smartest dog alive." Lester sped away, surprising Ollie, Bo, and Alvin.

"Everyone wanted Dolby to win, didn't they, Ollie? Even Lester. Dolby could have won, too."

"Look at it this way, Bo," Ollie pointed out. "Now that I've thought this over, it isn't a tragedy at all. Dolby didn't win the contest, but he's a hero. If Dolby hadn't answered the telephone, we wouldn't have been there for the call from the hospital. No one except Dolby would have heard that phone ringing way down the hall."

That was true, but it didn't make Bo feel any better. Dolby had lost. Bo had lost. This was their best chance, probably their only chance to be famous, and it hadn't worked out.

The boys took Truffles home. Afterward, at the Dibbses', Bo told Alvin the whole story again over a sandwich, a big slice of chocolate-pudding cake, and a glass of milk each. Dolby ate his Woofies. There was plenty of Woofies Dog Food and Woofies Snacks. Each dog had been sent a month's supply, just for being a finalist in the contest.

Mrs. Dibbs was too tired to cook that night, so she stopped at the supermarket after work and bought submarine sandwiches. No one was very hungry, though, especially Alice, who was excited about the dance.

At the dinner table, Bo told his mother the whole Dolby story. "So he didn't even get a chance to win the contest." Bo sighed again, thinking about it. He leaned his chin on his fist and swallowed the huge lump in his throat.

"I'm sorry, Bo," Mrs. Dibbs said, sipping her coffee. "Dolby's act was wonderful. 'The best laid schemes of mice and men . . .' "

"What do mice have to do with Dolby's tragedy?" asked Bo.

"Never mind," said Mrs. Dibbs. "It's just a saying."

After supper, Mrs. Dibbs told the boys they could watch the television news in case it showed the Woof-Off. While they watched, she turned on her favorite music station in the family room and worked on her very last jigsaw puzzle—she promised herself—until winter set in again. Alice was upstairs, getting ready for the dance. Dolby, who wasn't allowed on the living-room rug, lay stretched in the hall beside the carpet.

"There it is," Ollie said when the tape of the contest came on. "Look, there's Frank and Basher. Maybe Basher won."

The camera showed several of the dogs as they performed. More time was given to the Woof-Off than any other local news.

"Yeah, if Basher or Truffles won, I'd try to be glad," said Bo. He sat Indian-style, his elbows on his knees, fists on his chin. "Look, even Truffles made it on TV."

"Dr. Norbert was right." Ollie pointed. "That Great Dane did win. Look at him. He does look and sound great."

"Dolby would have been wonderful, too"—Bo glanced at his sleeping dog—"if he'd have had a chance."

"He had a chance," Ollie reminded Bo. "But he blew it."

"Yeah, Dolby, you blew it."

Dolby didn't seem too concerned. He did jump up, however, when the doorbell rang.

"Will you see who it is, Ollie?" Mrs. Dibbs said. "It's probably Hamilton. I'm too tired to move."

"Will you let Hamilton in, Bo?" said Ollie. "I want to watch this piece about those kids that are trying to get some changes made on that dangerous stretch of highway where some of their friends were killed."

Bo had seen all the news he wanted to see. He ran to the front door. He'd tell Hamilton who won while he waited for Alice to finish getting ready.

To Bo's surprise, the person at the Dibbses' front door wasn't Hamilton Byers. It wasn't anyone Bo knew. He was just getting ready to call his mother when the man spoke.

"Is this the home of Dolby Dibbs, the Wonder Dog?" The man smiled. "I'm a reporter from the *Daily Camera*. I'd like to interview Dolby."

12

Dolby, the Wonder Dog

"Who is it, Bo?" Mrs. Dibbs called when Bo and Hamilton Byers didn't come back into the living room.

"It's a reporter," Bo was finally able to say. "He wants to talk to Dolby."

Dolby had gone to the door with Bo. Now Mrs. Dibbs and Ollie joined them.

"A reporter?" Mrs. Dibbs questioned. "May I see some identification?"

"Yes, ma'am." He held out a card from his billfold. "May I come in?" The reporter took off his hat and looked at Dolby. "Isn't this the dog?"

"Well, yes, come in." Mrs. Dibbs stepped back, inviting the man into the living room. She snapped off the television and took a seat. "What do you want? Bo said Dolby was disqualified from the contest."

"I saw all that," said the reporter, who introduced himself as Roger Stearns. "I was covering the Woof-

Off. When I saw Dr. Norbert leave and the boys take Truffles, I smelled a bigger story than who won the contest. I've just come from the hospital, where I talked to Dr. Norbert. He was coming out of surgery. I got an even better story than I had hoped. Bo, did you know that you saved a little girl's eye?"

Bo didn't know any such thing. He couldn't speak.

"Could you explain this?" Mrs. Dibbs asked Roger Stearns.

"With an eye injury, time is very important. Dr. Norbert told me that his answering service knew he was at the contest, but that his pager didn't work. The operator called his home, but no one answered. Then she tried the school, hoping to somehow get a message to him. The first time she called, the phone was picked up, but there was some kind of weird interference. She tried again, and because you boys were there and took Dr. Norbert the message, he was able to get to the hospital in time for the emergency surgery."

"See, Bo," said Ollie, "I told you so. Dolby really is a hero."

"What I don't understand is why you boys were in the office. What caused you to answer the phone?" Roger Stearns had his pen ready for the answer.

"If you don't know, why did you ask for Dolby when you came to the door?" asked Bo.

The reporter laughed. "I saw Dolby's name in the program. I was being funny."

"It's not funny," Bo said. "Dolby's a hero. He is the Wonder Dog. Dolby answered the telephone."

Dolby, hearing his name, barked from his seat in the hallway.

"Your dog answered the phone?" Now Mr. Stearns seemed puzzled.

So Bo, helped by Ollie, told the reporter the whole story—how he'd taught Dolby to answer the phone as a special trick for the contest, how he'd had to untrain Dolby, but that Dolby remembered the trick during the finals of the Woof-Off.

"So that's why he ran out of the room when it was his turn to perform." Roger nodded. "I thought your dog was just misbehaving."

"No, *he* heard the phone. We didn't. Dolby's ears are tuned in to that kind of noise." Bo was starting to be proud of Dolby instead of disappointed.

"This gets better and better." Roger Stearns stood up after scribbling himself some notes. "May I see Dolby answer the phone, and take a picture?"

"Well, he's not supposed to do it anymore." Bo looked at his mother. "He's going to be really mixed up if we let him."

"Maybe one more time wouldn't hurt," said Mrs. Dibbs. "You can make him wait until you give him permission."

Bo called Alvin and asked him to phone right back. When the bell jangled, Dolby looked at Bo. There was a crowd in the kitchen by then.

"It's okay, Dolby," Bo said. "Answer the phone this time, just this one more time. It's all right."

When Dolby was sure, and the phone *brrrringed*

again, he stood up on the counter, lifted the receiver, laid it carefully on the floor, and barked. *"Woof-woof, wait a minute."* Then he looked at Bo and smiled, waiting for his Woofies Snack.

Not wanting to reward Dolby with food, Bo just went over and hugged the big dog tightly.

"Well, I'll be darned," said the reporter, who had snapped several photos of the event. "If you hadn't shown me this trick, I'd never have believed it. Do you mind if I take some more photos of Dolby, maybe doing his other tricks, the ones he didn't get to show us in the contest?"

Bo looked at his mother. She laughed, shrugged, and said, "Why not, Bo? Maybe it will make up for not winning the contest." She walked over and placed the teakettle on the stove, still shaking her head.

The reporter took many pictures of Dolby, sitting tall, playing dead, fetching, and woofing. Dolby loved the attention.

When the doorbell rang, no one paid attention, so Alice went downstairs herself. "I'm leaving, Mom," she called from the other room. "I don't even want to know what's going on in there."

"Will this be in tomorrow's paper?" Bo asked the reporter when he got ready to leave.

"I think so, Bo. I'm going right back to the office to develop this film and finish my story. Thanks for the great interview, Dolby."

"Woof-woof," barked Dolby. *"Woof-woof."*

Bo could hardly get to sleep that night. Dolby in the morning's paper—he could scarcely believe it.

Sure enough, the next day, right on the front page of the *Daily Camera* was a portrait of Dolby, his tongue lolling out one side of his mouth. There were smaller pictures on another page, where the story continued. One was of Dolby answering the phone, and one was of him fetching the toy kitten.

The headline read: DOLBY, THE WONDER DOG, GIVES UP HIS CHANCES IN THE WOOF-OFF TO HELP A CHILD.

"Dolby Dibbs, who belongs to the Dibbs family at 3991 Oakwood, gave up his chances on Saturday to win the highly publicized Woof-Off contest run by Woofies Dog Food," Ollie read. Bo sat listening closely to every word.

"Unselfishly, Dolby left the finals, disqualifying himself, to answer the telephone that was ringing in the office of the school. As chance would have it, the call was an emergency for Dr. Moe Norbert, a Boulder eye doctor, also showing his dog in the Woof-Off. Sheri Longholtz was playing—"

"Sheri Longholtz!" Bo said. "I didn't know it was Sheri."

"Sheri Longholtz," Ollie continued, "was playing with a baton, tossing it into the air at her home. Wearing sunglasses, which were not made of safety glass, proved unfortunate for the child. When the baton hit her in the face, the glasses broke. Shards of glass lodged in one eye, and she needed immediate attention. Dr. Norbert was able to get to the hospital in time, thanks to

Dolby. He reports that the girl's eye will recover nicely. The *Camera* would like to recognize Dolby Dibbs as dog hero of the year and say, 'Better luck next time, Dolby, in the Woof-Off. But thanks for your unselfish attention to duty as man's best friend.' "

"Good grief," said Alice, sipping her orange juice. "Was that what was going on when Hamilton came?" She went to look for a box of cereal. Sunday-morning breakfast at the Dibbses' was a help-yourself affair.

"I think the reporter did a good job on the story, don't you, Ollie?" Bo asked, staring at the picture of Dolby. He started reading the article again to himself.

Mrs. Dibbs came in, and Bo and Ollie read it aloud to her.

"Well, Dolby is certainly a hero, isn't he?" Mrs. Dibbs made herself a cup of coffee. "Your father is going to be surprised."

"My friends will never let me hear the end of this." Alice shoved wheat biscuits under her milk and let them pop up again.

When the phone rang, Dolby jumped immediately to his feet.

"No, Dolby, I'll get it," Ollie said, almost falling over the big dog. "You're untrained, remember?" Ollie listened, then handed the phone to Bo. "It's for you, Bo."

"Hello." Bo took the phone and patted Dolby on the head at the same time. "Hi, Sheri. Did you see the paper?" Bo listened for a few minutes, saying "Yeah" occasionally, then hung up.

"That was Sheri Longholtz. Her mother read her the

article in the paper. She wanted to say thanks. I'm glad you helped her, Dolby."

Bo thought of what Sheri had told him. She'd have to wear a patch now. But it would be only temporary, too, thanks to Dr. Norbert getting there in time.

Bo hadn't thought anything would make up for losing the Woof-Off, but now he changed his mind. It felt really good to know he had had a part in helping Sheri. After all, it had been his idea in the first place to teach Dolby to answer the phone. Now Dolby was a hero. Didn't that make Bo sort of a hero, too? His name was in the paper when it got to the part about training Dolby. That didn't exactly make him famous, but maybe there were better things than being famous.

"Good dog, Dolby." Bo patted Dolby on the head and nearly tripped over him getting into the cupboard. He poured Dolby's dish full of Woofies again. "You're my best friend, Dolby, my best friend in the whole world." Bo hugged Dolby.

Brrrring-brrring. The phone shrilled once more. Dolby looked at Bo. "No, Dolby. Forget about answering." Bo held Dolby's collar. Alice grabbed the phone.

"Good grief!" she said after listening a minute. She had a smile on her face. "This time it's for Dolby."

"For Dolby?" asked Bo. "Who is it?"

"I have no idea. Some of his fan club, I guess." Alice winked and handed the receiver to Bo.

"It's Dad," said Bo, listening. "He's calling all the way from Mexico to hear about the contest." Bo told Mr.

Dibbs part of the story. He'd save the rest for when his father got home. "Speak, Dolby, speak," Bo commanded, holding the phone near Dolby. "Give Dad your best woof."

Dolby looked at Bo. He looked at the phone. His tail thumped the kitchen floor.

"Yes, it's all right to speak, boy. Go ahead."

"Woof-woof," said Dolby. *"Woof-woof."*

"Good dog," said Bo. He gave his mom the phone. "Dolby, the Wonder Dog, wonders if everyone in town will want to talk to him and get his autograph."

Bo fell over laughing on the kitchen floor as Mom hung up and the Dibbses' phone jingled again.